INTO THE CRIMSON MIST

From the Tales of Orenda

Book Two

Gray Door Ltd.

First Edition © 2018 by Oliver Phipps

ISBN: 978-1-945530-94-4

CONTENTS

Chapter One:

IT BEGAN WITH A SWIM

"The drums played unwavering rhythms," Onsi began to pat his thighs in a drumming fashion, as a dozen young children sat in a semi-circle around him, staring wide-eyed, mouths agape.

"The rain came down, and thunder erupted. Lightning, again and again, lit up the embattled village." Onsi stopped patting his legs and stretched out his arms, then he let out a sudden thundering sound… "Whooombbbb!"

The children sat back, and a few young girls squealed.

Onsi became quiet, and all the young eyes became affixed on him.

"There… to the west… a huge female lofa was seen breaking into the village. She was enormous and had the black eyes of death." Pointing as if spotting a beast, Onsi then jumped back a bit. "Wait! There's another one coming from the other direction!"

The children gasped as Onsi became even more animated.

"Nazshoni drew her bow back and sent arrow after arrow to the vile beasts. But they continued to rampage and destroy huts. Several women were struck down as they chanted and hit their sticks together. Still, the drums and chants continued, bravely sounding out, giving our men strength of spirit in the deadly fight."

Smoke from a morning fire drifted through the gathering as Onsi repositioned himself and continued.

"Then, as we fought in the mud and rain, as our fires struggled to burn, as Orenda attacked with the courage of ten men, the male lofa charged into the area. He grabbed Orenda by the leg and ran, dragging the warrior out of the battle area. Nazshoni shouted and tried to follow, but a female lofa had her trapped, forcing her to stay and fight in the village.

"Deep into the woods, Orenda was pulled by the foul beast. His back and legs were scratched and battered, but he used his tomahawk to latch onto a tree, and this jerked him free from the lofa's grasp.

"Orenda stood as the large male turned and charged him. The warrior rolled away from the creature and was quickly back on his feet as the beast came back around for another strike."

Onsi smiled slightly as he noticed the children were all transfixed on this tale, one that he had told them at least fifty times before. He always tried to add things he'd forgotten about the battle or things Nazshoni and Lonato had told him about the fierce struggle between Orenda and the male lofa. But the story was still basically the same. Yet, here these youngsters were, eyes glistening with excitement and hanging upon his every word as if it were the first time they had heard the tale.

Onsi continued.

"As the beast readied himself for another charge, Orenda heard raspy breathing. The warrior realized the creature had indeed been struck by one of Nazshoni's snake arrows; it was sick, and this would be to his advantage.

"The beast charged again, and this time Orenda could not fall away fast enough. The lofa's claws raked against the warrior's arm, inflicting three large gashes into it."

Onsi raked three fingers on his own upper arm to indicate the lofa's strike. Then pointing up and into the area on his left, he went on.

"In the distance, Nazshoni and Lonato had finally arrived at the battlegrounds and watched from a small hill. Lonato found it necessary to hold Nazshoni tightly, or she would have dashed to her death in defense of her husband. Lonato told her they must not distract the great warrior lest he lose his focus.

"It was the right thing to do, as the lofa charged again and again."

Orenda approached the gathering, and realizing Onsi was telling a story, he stopped, smiled, and waited for him to finish the tale. The warrior watched as the children's faces expressed excitement and intrigue.

After a few minutes, Onsi finished the now-famous story concerning the battle with the fierce lofa.

A hush fell over the group as the children appeared to be spellbound by the tale. Then, from behind them, Orenda walked up.

The youngsters turned to the warrior and examined him in awe. He looked the group over briefly and noticed all the children's eyes were fixed upon the three scars on his arm. After smiling and nodding to them, he turned back to Onsi.

"Uhm, Onsi, I hate to disturb your activities with the children, but I need to talk if you have time."

Onsi stood. "That will be fine. I've just finished telling them a story."

He glanced down to the children, "If you youngsters will excuse us for a while, I'll tell you another tale tonight."

The children smiled and were soon moving to different areas of the village.

Orenda watched as some went into their families' mud huts, and others found their parents or siblings and began helping with various chores.

He then turned to Onsi, who was observing the warrior.

"So, you told them a tale of the lofa again?"

Orenda then began to walk, and Onsi followed.

"They continue to ask for it. What am I to do?"

Orenda smiled slightly as they moved past a small fire that several women were using to cook a morning meal.

A chill still held the air as the two men walked, but the spring sun was slowly warming the day.

"It seems they would tire of that story by now. You've been telling it all winter."

"Well, they've already heard the old stories that everyone else has heard. Other than a few short tales that I've pried from Nazshoni and Kanuna, it's the only new story I've got to tell. You're a great warrior, Orenda. The children wish to know more about you. If you would share a few of your adventures with me, I could brighten the children's day with new tales."

Orenda stopped and looked at Onsi. He seemed to be considering the request. Then he started walking again.

"I'm a warrior, my friend, not a storyteller. And, I don't think we would have the time for additional stories anyway as our departure day grows near."

By this time, the two had ventured to the edge of the village. In the distance, they could see a massive waterway, which the white man called the "Mississippi River."

"Have you learned the various languages from the teachers?" Orenda asked.

"Yes, I've learned all the teachers instructed me to learn."

"Good, then you should begin to pack your things. We'll be crossing the great river as soon as the weather clears a bit more. We must get to the other side and travel far if there is to be any hope of reaching our destination before winter returns."

Onsi nodded, and Orenda turned and walked back toward the village. Onsi continued to stare at the massive river in the distance.

It had been almost a year since the four had left his village. The memories of their battle with the lofa now seemed almost surreal.

A breeze caressed his face as he recalled his long journey to find the legendary warrior. Then he remembered the hopelessness that had held his people as he, Orenda, his wife Nazshoni, and her brother Kanuna entered the village.

Their faces expressed the exhaustive struggle and loss of friends and family they had endured. The lofa had been feeding on the village for many months.

He recalled the violent battles and finally the victory over the beasts. It had indeed been the "bitter harvest," Orenda spoke of.

Onsi turned and walked back toward the village. He had desperately wanted to accompany the warriors, and they eventually agreed he could journey with them.

As he swatted the tiny green buds of a bush along the trail, he considered the life he now faced. He knew it would be challenging.

The four had been invited to stay with this village, which Chief Hakane had directed them to lodge the winter with. They had been learning different languages of tribes on the western side of the river. Many were like his own language and not difficult to learn. A few took more time to become proficient. Yet, he had learned well. Now, the unknown future brought a familiar feeling to his very soul, the feeling of unease—the feeling he felt as he had waited for the vicious lofa to cross the ravine and attack.

Onsi stopped and looked at the dwellings ahead of him. He pushed the feelings back down to the depths of his being, straightening up, and moved on toward the community.

Meanwhile, in a small mud hut located on the edge of the village, Orenda spoke with his wife, Nazshoni.

"I told Onsi to start packing. I also asked about his language skills. He expressed confidence in what he's learned over the winter."

Nazshoni watched her husband as he lifted his musket and inspected it. He then glanced at her.

"What are you thinking, my wife?"

"Do you feel he's ready? I know he asked to come with us, and I know we all agreed to let him. But he might still have a normal life. If you told him to stay, he could remain here and find a wife. He's become so fond of the children, and they love him as well." She paused and rubbed her hands together. Then continued. "I'm just afraid… Well, I know what we've faced before and will face in the future. Do you really feel he's ready for that?"

Orenda leaned the musket against the wall of the hut. He considered Nazshoni's words and then replied as a small fire shed a dim light on his face.

"Onsi has fought the lofa. I can imagine few things worse to face in battle than a pack of such vile beasts. He is a grown man. He knows what path he wishes to follow, and we should respect that. We didn't ask him to come with us. We offered that path, and he chose it willingly."

Nazshoni took in a deep breath and then expelled it slowly.

"I just worry about him. I wonder if bringing him along was the right thing." She then looked at her husband again.

Orenda smiled. "You now know how I've felt about the decision to bring you and Kanuna along with me. I still worry about you both and often wonder if I made the right choice."

His wife expressed a new understanding. Her mouth twisted slightly, and she examined the fire.

Orenda came over and ran his hand through her long black hair.

"We can't foresee all of the challenges ahead. But I know Onsi wants to do something good, as we all do. He should have the opportunity to help those in need. That feeling of helping others will always be worth the struggle if it's what we truly desire. I feel in Onsi's heart, he truly desires that."

Nazshoni looked up to her husband, smiled, and took his hand in hers.

The following week, Orenda decided the weather was right, and they prepared to leave.

The people of the village came to them, expressing sorrow that the visitors were departing. Orenda, Nazshoni, Kanuna, and Onsi had lived with them through the long winter. The village elders had taught each one as many languages and words of other tribes as they could during this time. They also taught them all they knew concerning what the four would face on the other side of the great river.

During their stay, skilled canoe makers prepared an additional number of large devices to get the warriors and their horses across the expansive waterway. Although these villagers were experienced in crossing the great river, they had never taken a group of people and horses the size of Orenda's.

The children gathered around Onsi, and some wept while saying their goodbyes. As the morning sun warmed the ground, the four mounted their horses and, with pack animals in tow, began to follow several men of the village as they rode toward the area that had been prepared for the crossing.

While riding along the well-worn path, Onsi moved up beside Kanuna. He had gained much respect for the young warrior, who was not much older than himself. He often asked Kanuna things that he would be too afraid to ask Orenda or Nazshoni.

"I've been wondering."

Kanuna turned his attention to Onsi.

"What have you been wondering?"

"Well, I know we're on our way to fight giants…somewhere far away. But I wondered how the people managed to find Orenda and gain his pledge of support."

Kanuna studied Onsi as they both swayed slightly to the movement of their mounts.

Onsi became concerned with Kanuna's reluctance to reply. He continued.

"What I mean is, it took me an entire season to find you three. And, my village was much closer than where we seem to be going. I know Orenda's fame spreads across great distances, but it still makes me wonder."

Kanuna turned his attention back to the path. He remained quiet for several long seconds. Onsi again became concerned that he had asked too much.

Finally, to Onsi's relief, Kanuna answered him.

"No one found Orenda. He had several spirit dreams. In these dreams, he traveled far and saw giants and the people they were tormenting. He knows where they are, and he knows we are the only ones who can help them."

Onsi struggled with this revelation for several minutes as they rode alongside the river. Then he asked Kanuna, "Do you believe the dreams?"

The young warrior examined Onsi and replied, "If Orenda believes the dreams, I believe them."

Onsi nodded, and the two returned their attention to the trail.

After a lengthy ride, they arrived at a river inlet. Here the men from the village helped unload the horse's packs and saddles. They then began hooking up canoes to both sides of the animals. They did this by positioning the horses between platforms made of poles. The canoes rested on the platforms. No weight was placed on the animals until after the ropes and leather harnesses had been attached securely.

Once the canoes were fastened to each side of a horse, the animal was led to the water, and once in, the canoes were loaded with the warrior's belongings.

Eventually, all eight horses were tied together with a length of rope and were floating in the inlet.

Nazshoni and Orenda came to Onsi.

"There are still a few villages of your Chickasaw tribe on the other side of the river," Nazshoni said. "But we will likely leave those tribes behind within a few weeks."

Onsi studied her as she said this. He suddenly feared that they were about to send him back to his home village. Nazshoni continued.

"Where we're going is very far, Onsi. It's doubtful that we will ever come back here. Are you sure that you wish to continue?"

Orenda watched Onsi but gave no expression as to his thoughts. Nazshoni had concern in her eyes.

Onsi thought about never returning. He felt his heart beating faster as he contemplated what may lay ahead. But he quickly replied.

"You're my family now. I will go where you go. Your battles are my battles. I may not be a strong warrior, but I will do everything I can to help us win the fight."

Nazshoni smiled, and Orenda appeared happy with Onsi's reply.

"All right, let's go then," the warrior said, and they were soon swimming out to the horses. After a few minutes, each one had climbed into a canoe.

The village men, who had experience crossing the river, occupied the lead horses and canoes. They began moving the group slowly out to the large waterway.

Carefully, the string of man and beasts moved across the expanse of moving water. The horses initially struggled but soon became weary and allowed the floating devices to carry them across.

Occasionally, Onsi would glance back from where they had come. The home of his childhood and now his very tribe were fading in the distance.

The sun was past the midday sky before the group finally arrived on the west side of the great river. Once the rigging and canoes were removed from the horses, the band of warriors began to repack their belongings.

One of the village men approached Orenda. Though Onsi was placing items on a packhorse, he overheard the conversation.

"There will be a few more Chickasaw villages west of here. But you will soon venture into the unknown lands. You should take care as there have been stories of dark lakes and shadow magic. They may only be stories, but something caused them to be told."

Orenda thanked the villager and continued his task of preparing for the journey.

The village men tied the canoes together and were soon making their way back across the massive waterway.

"So, how long before we find these, giants?" Onsi asked, attempting to sound confident as he attached equipment to his packhorse.

Orenda glanced back at him.

"I doubt we will find them before winter. It's very far."

Nazshoni watched Onsi for a reaction as she tightened the saddle straps on her horse.

Soon the group was riding west, along a barely visible path.

That evening, they made camp, and after a meal, Orenda smoked his pipe as Nazshoni combed his long black hair.

Kanuna carved a delicate pattern into a piece of wood he had picked up during the day.

Onsi watched the others and poked at the fire with a stick, as this had become his chosen activity after the meals.

The following day, they were up before dawn and soon heading west again. In this manner, the days began to blur together.

It had been months since they had traveled in this manner. But, day by day, they settled back into a regular routine and the soreness of riding for long stretches of time became less and less noticeable.

Chapter Two:

VILLAGE OF THE DEAD

On several occasions, the four came to small Chickasaw villages. The people immediately welcomed the visitors after Onsi introduced Orenda. They had heard of the battles with the lofa and quickly prepared a grand meal for the travelers.

Yet, as the days turned into weeks, they soon journeyed far beyond the boundaries of Onsi's tribe. The surroundings began to appear strange, and new sounds entered the adventurers' ears. Animals and birds they were not familiar with could be detected in the formidable woods that surrounded them.

Day after day, they moved farther and farther westward. Every week that went by, the environment grew less familiar. Oddly, they saw no person or village. It seemed as if they had left the known world and were now in an area completely uninhabited by people.

Then, suddenly and unexpectedly, they came upon a frightening sight.

Orenda stopped, and soon the others came up to him and stared at a thing such as they had never seen before.

A skeleton was attached by ropes to a tree. It seems the person had been tied there years ago since the bones were bare and bleached from the sun.

What the travelers found most unnerving was the skull. Two sharpened sticks had been inserted into the eye sockets. Since they were also driven into the tree, the four concluded these sticks had, very possibly, been driven into the person's eyes while he or she was alive.

After studying the odd find for a few moments, Orenda turned his horse west, and the journey resumed.

As they continued, they began to spot deer skulls, which were tied to trees as well. These had been hanging for several years at least, as they were bleached by the sun.

Strangely, many of the deer skulls had sticks driven into the eye sockets, just as the human skull had.

Onsi felt a chill run up his spine and tried to push down his wariness.

That night, Orenda appeared deep in thought as he smoked his pipe. Onsi watched him from across the dying fire. None had asked about the odd skulls, and Onsi held back a desire to do so. Finally, the group lay down to sleep.

The following morning, Onsi noticed that Nazshoni had changed from her dress to a set of buckskin breeches and top that she wore when fighting. She also had her bow and quiver of arrows on her back.

As they prepared to depart the campsite, Onsi readied his tomahawk on the saddle where he could easily reach it if needed.

Before the sun hit a midday sky, the travelers wandered into an even stranger find.

As they approached what looked to be a village, the ground became desolate of life. Dead trees littered the area, with bare limbs hanging down ominously.

Riding into the midst of time-weathered mud huts, they realized the structures had been abandoned for many seasons.

Orenda stopped in the middle of the ghost village and dismounted. The others did likewise.

Tying his horse to the protruding framework of a vacant hut, he patted his mount on the neck and then pulled a tomahawk from his gear.

Nazshoni readied her bow. Kanuna and Onsi also prepared their weapons as their leader began to look around.

The three followed Orenda as he examined the inside of several huts. Kanuna came up to him cautiously as they approached another time-battered structure.

"Do you think a sickness came to this village?" Kanuna asked as Orenda glanced into the hut.

"A sickness didn't do that," Orenda said.

Kanuna turned and investigated the hut. Inside was another skeleton. This person had also been tied up with ropes and had sticks embedded into the eye sockets.

The young warrior grimaced slightly as he then turned to follow Orenda, who had started walking again.

Nazshoni and Onsi both quickly examined the skeleton as they passed by.

After moving through the ghost village, finding nothing but skeletons with sticks where the eyes would have been, they returned to their horses.

Orenda and the others untied their mounts. The warrior then gazed around at the desolate surroundings. A dusty breeze flowed through the area, carrying bits of dried foliage with it.

"This place met a very unusual death," Orenda said and then continued. "Not only the people, but the very ground itself has died."

Onsi glanced down at the barren soil and then quickly mounted his horse as he noticed Orenda, and the others were doing.

Two days later, and around two months after crossing the great river, they came to a large, low-water area. Trees grew up inside the expanse of black water. Grass and roots hung down from the branches, creating a strange and ominous sight. Orenda maneuvered his horse north and then south. He moved from shallow area to shallow area. Soon, they were surrounded by the swamps and dark water.

After a day filled with slow, arduous travel, they found a somewhat dry area and made camp.

The night became black as the group sat around the fire, eating their evening meal. Onsi gazed nervously into the darkness as many strange sounds echoed all around them.

After the meal, they followed their regular routine but were constantly distracted by large splashes and loud cries from birds and beasts of which Onsi had little or no knowledge.

"I wonder how much more... What did you call it, Orenda?"

Onsi glanced at Orenda as Nazshoni gently combed his hair.

The warrior expelled a long draw of smoke. He leaned the long stem pipe on his leg and looked over to Onsi.

"Do you mean, 'swamp?'"

"Yes, that's what you called it. And what about those large lizard creatures you spoke of, which often live in swamps?"

"Alligators?" Orenda asked, seeming a bit amused by Onsi's apprehension.

"Oh, yes, that's right, alligators." He studied Orenda briefly and then glanced back into the darkness with obvious unease.

"How is it you're familiar with those beasts?" he finally asked after hearing another large splash in the distance.

Orenda again expelled a draw of smoke as Nazshoni began to tie his hair back.

"I spent some time with the Seminoles. There was a period in my younger days when I wandered about. It was with the Seminoles that I learned of swamps and alligators."

Onsi smiled nervously. "Well, I'm glad you know about such things.... Do alligators, uhm, eat people?"

Nazshoni stopped her activity and glanced at Onsi. Her eyes closed slightly as she rather obviously held back a smile, then proceeded to finish tying her husband's hair back.

Orenda considered the question. He tapped his spent pipe on a log at the edge of the fire. Then he replied, "I've heard they enjoy the taste of short, nervous Chickasaw men."

With this remark, Nazshoni and Kanuna laughed aloud. Onsi grimaced slightly but then also began to laugh, as did Orenda.

The following day, they again carefully traversed the swamp.

After almost a week of difficult travel, they began to emerge from the shallow lake area. Just as they did so, Orenda stopped abruptly.

As the others gathered around, they noticed why he had stopped and what he was now looking at.

Hanging on a tree was a large male deer head. The hide was stretched and coming apart, but this one appeared to be only one season old. What stood out more than anything were the eyes. There were no sticks in this one's eyes. Instead, the deer's eyes had been covered with a black clay-like substance. Over this black substance were eyes painted on with white paint.

Orenda studied the odd find for several long seconds before Kanuna commented.

"This was done more recently and surely by people." He examined the deer head for a few more seconds before continuing. "I was beginning to think the few people who lived around here died in the abandoned village."

Orenda's horse moved under him as if nervous. The warrior patted his mount on the neck to calm it. Without replying, he turned the horse west and continued.

Onsi's face twisted a bit as he moved past the deer head. He tried to imagine who would make such a thing.

Again, they maneuvered cautiously through the dense woodland. A short time later, Orenda again stopped. Once more, there was a deer head hanging on the side of a tree. Again, the eyes had been filled with the black clay-like substance and white eyes painted over the black areas.

The warrior glanced back at the others, seeming to consider their expressions. He then turned his mount and again moved west.

A path soon presented itself, and after Orenda decided to follow it, the way became less difficult to traverse.

Cautiously, the group moved through the woods. Initially, birds were heard singing in the trees. But, as they moved farther along the trail, the birds could no longer be heard.

By midday, the four travelers moved in almost silence. From time to time, they looked to each other as the strange lack of natural sounds in the woodlands made all four weary.

Along the trail, they passed several more of the odd deer heads. Orenda no longer stopped to study them, but as they moved by, all four examined the ominous items curiously.

Chapter Three:

THE LANDS OF CHAK-RAH

As the sun crested and slowly began to move west, the four were surprised to come upon a man sitting on a large rock. He wore a cougar hide, and the head of the cougar rested on the top of his own head. He was leaned over, grinding something, perhaps herbs, in a makeshift pestle. The cougar head faced the travelers and stared at them as they approached.

Onsi thought the man might be deaf as he continued his work for several long seconds after the group arrived in front of him and had all come to a stop.

Orenda said nothing but watched the odd bobbing of the cougar head that seemed to watch the travelers with dead eyes.

Behind the man was a crude lean-to and campfire. Smoke drifted through the visitors' ranks, and the sun beat down upon them, causing a glistening of sweat on all.

Finally, the man spoke, though he did not raise his head.

"These are perilous times for unwary travelers to venture into the lands of Chak-Rah. Are you perhaps lost?"

The man then looked up to the group. His face had black paint across the eyes and streaming down the side of his cheeks to end in a point at the lower portion of his jaw. He also looked to be in his mid-fifties.

Orenda studied the man briefly before replying.

"Perilous times, you say? A warning from an old shaman sitting casually on a rock, making potions. Other than a dead village and strange signs along the way, we've not noticed any perilous situations."

The old shaman examined the four carefully. Then he replied.

"Warriors from the east..." He stood and stepped down from the large rock, then moved over to Orenda.

"Not just any warriors. No...not misguided adventurers, or lost treasure seekers."

He examined the scars on Orenda's arm. He then turned and looked over to Nazshoni with increasing interest and excitement.

"No, this is the Storm Rider and his wife." The old shaman backed up and looked the two over again.

Orenda glanced at Nazshoni. Behind them, Kanuna looked at Onsi as if to be sure they had not become invisible.

"You are the one called Orenda, the Storm Rider; killer of beasts. You are the warrior who defeated Blood Hawk in battle, the vanquisher of the demon soldiers. Among other brave deeds that I've heard. That is, you?"

Orenda shifted in his saddle, seeming uncomfortable with the lengthy accolades.

"Yes, that is me...." Orenda was immediately interrupted by the old shaman before he could continue.

"And your wife..." The shaman turned to Nazshoni. "She is said to be a fierce warrior. The stories indicate she fought bravely against Blood Hawk's warriors and killed the lofa as well. It is said she is a bowwoman with skills greater than most male warriors."

Nazshoni's mouth twisted slightly, and she shifted in her saddle, also seeming uncomfortable.

"You seem to know much about us. But we know little of you," Orenda said with a tone of impatience.

The old man glanced back to Orenda.

"Who I am is of little importance. I am simply an old shaman endeavoring to amend a wrong. Chak-Rah destroyed my village. I have pursued her here. But I do not have the power to defeat her. Now, the providence of the Great Spirit has sent you and your wife to perhaps help bring balance back to these desolate lands."

Onsi noticed Kanuna's face twist in frustration. He said nothing but leaned upon the saddle horn as if becoming even more relaxed.

"I don't know of this Chak-Rah, and I have no quarrel with her. I'm sorry about your village, but we have a task beyond here, and we must continue on." Orenda then reined his horse to the left and began to move around the shaman's rough campsite.

As the others began to follow their leader, the old shaman said, "I understand... but I'm afraid the deer woman is already aware of you. She will not allow you to escape her grasp so easily."

Orenda stopped immediately. He then turned his horse back around.

The shaman climbed back up to his rock and sat down. As he was about to return to his task of grinding herbs, Orenda spoke.

"The deer woman? She is real then?"

"Yes, she is real. She is already aware of your presence. She has eyes all around her territory. I'm afraid your task will have to wait. The deer woman will certainly wish to meet the Storm Rider. No man can resist her. You, too, will soon find yourself in the blood mist."

The shaman then returned to his task of grinding herbs.

Nazshoni looked at Orenda with concern in her eyes.

"Thank you for the warning, old shaman. We'll move around her territory and tread lightly."

The old man simply nodded, the cougar head bobbing up and down, seeming to answer for him. He continued his task as if desiring no more conversation.

Orenda then proceeded around the campsite and began moving south rather than west.

Nazshoni rode close to Orenda.

"The deer woman, what do you know of her?"

Orenda glanced back as if to be sure Nazshoni was the only one who heard his words.

"Not much. I thought most, if not all, of what I heard to be stories meant to entertain children."

He shifted in his saddle and once again glanced cautiously back to the other two. He then continued.

"It's been said she is some type of "form or shapeshifter." She can take the form of animals. It's also been said she does not age and that she has some sort of power over men."

Nazshoni expressed even more concern. Orenda continued.

"But we don't have time to get tangled in such a thing. We'll go around this place and then move west again."

This seemed to calm Nazshoni. Orenda then spurred his mount to move faster, and the others quickened their pace as well.

As they traveled, more of the deer heads were spotted in the trees. Orenda noticed they appeared to be watching the group with their black and white eyes. He again coaxed his horse to a faster pace.

They continued through the woods with only the sounds of their horses' movements to be heard. No birds sang, and even the subtle breeze made little noise in the trees.

Suddenly, four deer came from nowhere and jumped in front of the group. This startled the horses, and several reared up. The four reigned in their mounts and halted as Orenda patted his horse's neck to calm it.

From the direction the deer came, riders burst through the woodland. There were ten of them, and they were in pursuit of the deer. As they saw Orenda and the others, they quickly abandoned the deer and, turning their mounts, came back toward the group.

Nazshoni had an arrow in her bow before the riders were completely turned. Orenda pulled the tomahawks from his saddle pack, as did Kanuna. Onsi had been so startled by the deer, he was left empty-handed by the time the riders came back with bows pulled tight and arrows pointed at the travelers.

The riders circled the group, and Onsi immediately noticed they were all young men. The oldest looked to be seventeen and the youngest thirteen.

Nazshoni had her arrow sighted upon the eldest, seeming to instinctively identify him as the leader.

For several long seconds, the two groups stared at each other with apprehension. Finally, the oldest boy spoke.

"Who are you, and what are you doing in our lands? We need no more trouble with strangers."

Orenda replied, "We are simply passing through. We're headed west and will not cause any trouble to you or your lands."

The boy's faces grew taught, and Onsi could tell they were having trouble holding their arrows in a ready state.

"That's not good enough! You will come with us! You must explain yourself to our chief!"

The boy's voice quivered slightly as he continued to hold the bow pointed at Orenda.

"We have no matters to discuss with your chief. As I said, we're merely passing through. Now, stow your weapons, and we'll be on our way."

The face of the leader twisted as he gripped the arrow tighter to keep it from taking flight.

"You'll die if you do not do as I say! Now, you stow your weapons and come with us!"

Nazshoni shouted, "You'll die if you don't do as you're told...boy!"

Anger came quickly to the leader's face, and with a quick move, he shifted his aim from Orenda to Nazshoni.

"Then we'll die together!" the leader shouted.

Onsi began to feel ill as it seemed someone was surely about to die. To do something, hopefully helpful, he shouted, "Show some respect for Orenda, the Storm Rider!"

All ten of the young men turned their attention to Onsi. But the leader did lower his bow and arrow, which gave Onsi a slight bit of satisfaction.

All the young men then lowered their weapons and examined the scars on Orenda's arm. A few seconds later, they began to whoop and shout as if excited but also a bit frightened.

As the young men shouted out, they began to move their horses about in a nervous manner. Onsi noticed that Nazshoni still held her bow and arrow trained on the young leader who threatened her husband. Onsi was again astonished by the bowwoman's strength and resolve.

Gradually, the young men calmed, and the leader spoke. As he had already lowered his bow and arrow, Nazshoni slowly lowered her weapon as well.

"You must come and speak with our chief. We are in a desperate situation, and he will wish to speak to the great Storm Rider."

"As I told you, we have no matter with you or your chief. We have matters to attend farther west. We must be on our way."

The young man's face became stern.

"As I've told you, our village is in a desperate situation. If I let you leave without speaking to our chief, I'll lose my honor."

The young leader stiffened up and continued. "I'll beg you if I must. But it will be necessary to kill me if that does not work."

From the side, another young man said, "You'll then have to kill me as well."

After this, all the other young men stated the same, that they would also need to be killed if Orenda did not agree to speak with the chief.

Orenda looked around at the young men. He took a deep breath of warm air into his lungs and then looked to his wife as he expelled it.

Nazshoni said nothing, but seeming to quickly weigh the options, she returned her arrow to the quiver and stowed her bow. Orenda then grimaced a bit but motioned toward the young man to lead the way.

Turning northwest, the travelers began to follow the young men.

After a while, they stopped. Orenda watched as the young leader dismounted, moved over to a tree, and cut down one of the odd deer heads. Once it was on the ground, the young man took an arrow, poked out the blackened eyes, then turned the eyes and face of the skull to the ground and covered the head with brush and leaves.

As he was remounting his horse, Orenda asked, "What are those things?"

The young man turned northwest again and answered, "They are the eyes of Chak-Rah. It's of little use to pull them down, as she has them all over our lands. But it is one of the few things we can do. It gives us a small amount of satisfaction in defying her."

As they rode along a now obvious trail, Orenda asked:

"Chak-Rah, she is the deer woman?"

"Yes, she came to our lands two years ago. The animals first became her slaves. Then the men of our village became her servants."

He glanced at Orenda with apparent apprehension and continued, "Our chief should be telling you this, not me."

Orenda nodded and returned his attention to the trail.

Soon, they entered a flat area with a variety of mud huts scattered about. Smoke greeted them from an unseen campfire. As they rode into the village, it appeared vacant and void of life. There were no sounds, only smoke and huts.

Finally, after passing numerous dwellings, some being in a state of disrepair, Orenda noticed a woman and several small children peeking from the doorway of their home. They then quickly disappeared back into the darkness.

The group stopped in front of a large hut. The young leader dismounted just as a very old man stepped out.

Orenda and the others dismounted as well.

The elderly man had the elaborate dress of a chief. He also used a walking stick that had a large claw from a bird of prey attached to the top.

The young warrior stepped up to his chief.

"My chief, we lost track of the deer, but we found someone you must surely wish to speak with."

The elderly chief studied Orenda and the others with curiosity, his eyes filled with a mix of pain and wisdom.

The young leader continued, "Chief Mulimo, this is the warrior Orenda...the Storm Rider."

Immediately, the chief straightened, and his face expressed interest and hope.

"The Storm Rider—we have heard stories of you. The Great Spirit must have surely brought you to us in our time of need," Mulimo replied with a raspy and weathered voice.

"We are honored to meet you, Chief Mulimo. I don't know that we can be of much assistance, but perhaps if we know more about your situation."

After Orenda said this, the elderly chief nodded and motioned for them to enter his hut.

The young men took the travelers' horses as Orenda, Nazshoni, Kanuna, and Onsi stepped into the chief's hut.

A dark smoky interior opened to the four as Chief Mulimo sat across from a small, smoldering fire in the middle of the dwelling.

"It's good that our warriors found you," the chief said once he was seated.

"Warriors?" Nazshoni asked as she also sat down.

"They are all we have left—ten young men. We decided any of our young under the age of thirteen should not be put into such a situation. Even though we have several of the age twelve and younger, who are very eager to protect the village."

"Where are all the men?" Orenda asked.

"She has them. They are blind to anything other than her commands. She took the strongest and bravest first. Then, as others attempted to rescue those, she took them. Now, we are a village of women, old men, and children. We can only hope she does not come for our young warriors. They must now hunt and provide, such as they can."

"Please tell us all you know about Chak-Rah," Orenda said.

The old chief nodded.

"She is a shapeshifter. She can change forms. It's been said she is hundreds of years old. As the story goes, her ancestors were all master shamans and shapeshifters. Her bloodline is ancient, and most feel she is a descendant of a long-lost tribe.

"Her father was said to be very skilled in the arts of a shaman. She learned her skills from him, and both used them for the good of their people."

An elderly woman entered the hut with a large water-skin and five cups. She began pouring the chief and then the visitors some water as Mulimo continued.

"She fell in love with a very handsome warrior; he was strong and courageous. However, the warrior did not love her. She began to use her magic to increase her desirability as a woman. Soon, many men were pursuing her. Yet, the man she loved began to court another woman.

"Her father became upset with her and tried to discipline his daughter. But she had become obsessed with her love for the warrior.

"As she delved deeper into the dark arts, her magic increased, yet it was evil in nature. She became enraged when the warrior announced his engagement to the woman he loved.

"In desperation, Chak-Rah changed into a deer and waited until the warrior's wife-to-be was alone. She then chased the woman until she fell into a snake pit and died from venomous bites.

"Chak-Rah then changed her form to that of the warrior's dead wife-to-be.

"This failed, however, as the warrior soon discovered it was not his true love. When he found the woman he loved to be dead, he attacked Chak-Rah in a fit of rage.

"This forced her to change form, and the entire village realized her foul deeds. In the form of a large deer, she killed the warrior with a strike of her hoof to his head.

"At this time, her father tried to intervene. But she cast a spell on him, and he was forced into the shape of a large bird. It seems he tried and tried but could not change back to human form and flew from the village.

"The villagers attacked, and she killed many of them. In the fight, fires broke out, and once night fell, there was little left.

"From that time, she has wandered. We think she uses the lives of men to prolong her own life. They slowly grow weaker, while she grows stronger."

Orenda and the other three considered the chief's tale. After a few minutes, Orenda asked, "Do you know where she is?"

"Yes... Well, we can find her. But it's dangerous to go near her lair. If you're sure you wish to go there, I'll have our warriors take you close enough to see where she is. But, I cannot ask them to go there. They are all we have left."

"I understand. If you can provide us a place to sleep tonight, we'll go in the morning."

Orenda paused and rubbed his chin, then continued.

"As I said, I don't know that we can do much. This is powerful magic, and we are not shamans. But we can at least look at her lair. Perhaps there is something we can do."

The old chief nodded.

"Yes, certainly we will provide you with food and a place to sleep. And, we understand that there may be little you can do. It's a burden that has fallen on us. We have known for some time now there is very little that can oppose this vile woman. Yet, we linger in the hope that something will free our loved ones from her grasp."

As the sun settled on the horizon, the four were led to a hut. After inspecting the inside, they decided to sleep outside where the breeze would cool them.

They started a small fire in a pit located in front of the hut. Several women came around with a meal. These women appeared very weary.

One woman of around twenty-five years old handed Orenda a dish with cooked venison. She then spoke with a stressed voice. "Please save my husband.... Please... I beg you." She then slipped away and around one of the huts.

Onsi began to feel as he did before he set out to find Orenda. His own village had been plagued by evil, and now he sensed the same hopelessness that his people had endured.

Orenda glanced at the plate of food and then looked at the other three, who were watching him. His expression was one of searching for something. Yet, the other three also felt lost as to what could be done.

"I fear this is something beyond our abilities," Orenda finally said. "My heart is heavy for these people, but magic cannot be defeated with tomahawks and arrows." He then began to eat, as did the others.

After a few moments, he continued.

"This, deer woman, she can change her form. This is very strong medicine. We'll go look at her lair tomorrow. There's no harm in that. But we should avoid a battle that we're sure to lose."

Onsi felt his heart sink. He finished his bite of food and asked meekly, "But, we will take a good look? Just in case there is something we can do for these people?"

Nazshoni's face expressed compassion as she belayed an understanding of Onsi's reason for asking such a thing. She then turned to Orenda as the darkness took over and light from the flames danced around them.

Orenda glanced down at his plate again. He seemed sad but then looked back to Onsi.

"Yes, we'll take a good look tomorrow...from a distance. Perhaps there is something we can do."

Onsi smiled very slightly, then lowered his head and focused on his meal, as did the others.

Later, the four made their beds around the fire pit. The bowwoman lay down by her husband, and soon all were asleep.

Chapter Four:

A THIEF IN THE NIGHT

A breeze caressed Nazshoni's face as she slept. She shifted over slightly and felt Orenda beside her.

Then, another breeze crossed her face, and this time there was an odd odor in it.

She opened her eyes, and fear gripped the depths of her being. A man leaned over toward her, yet his eyes were black as the deer heads they had seen along their journey. In the middle of this black clay substance, white eyes were painted and now stared at her.

The strange man held his hand open, with palm and fingertips pointed to Nazshoni's face. Before she could do anything, the black-eyed man blew on his hand, and an odd glowing dust went straight to her face and nose. She inhaled and immediately became a petrified person.

As the man moved back away from her, Nazshoni could see Orenda laying face up next to her. His eyes stared blankly into the sky.

With her heart beating fiercely but unable to move otherwise, the woman warrior noticed a red mist all around the area. Her eyes searched as far as she could see.

In the distance, men were barely visible at the edge of the mist. The black clay substance also covered their real eyes, and white eyes were painted over them.

As she was straining to see what was happening, a woman moved over to her. She was one of the most beautiful women Nazshoni had ever seen. Yet, on her head, she wore an odd piece that was fashioned of deer antlers. The woman appeared to be in her mid-twenties, around the same age as Nazshoni, and the bowwoman knew this must be the one called Chak-Rah.

The deer woman moved even closer to Nazshoni. She looked closely at her face. Then, a red mist enveloped Chak-Rah, and Nazshoni could not see the woman for a few seconds. As the mist cleared, Nazshoni was shocked to see her own face.

The warrior woman struggled with all her might to scream, or move, anything. Yet, she remained frozen.

The deer woman had changed and now looked identical to Nazshoni. She reached over to her and gently put a finger on her mouth. Then, she said to Nazshoni, "Speak softly."

Nazshoni immediately tried to yell, but her voice could only come out naturally and calmly.

"I'll kill you.... I'll kill you. What have you done to my husband?"

The deer woman said, "Ssshhhh," then touched her lips again, and Nazshoni could no longer speak.

Then Chak-Rah said in the same voice as Nazshoni, "I'll kill you.... I'll kill you. What have you done to my husband?"

Chak-Rah then moved over to Orenda, who still lay staring at the sky. She poured glimmering dust into her hand and, gently leaning over, blew the dust into Orenda's face.

"Wake up, my love. Let us leave here," Chak-Rah said to Orenda, but in the voice of Nazshoni. Orenda blinked but still appeared to be under some type of spell.

The warrior then took Chak-Rah's hand and stood up, never taking his eyes from the deer woman.

Nazshoni thought her heart would burst in her chest. She could do nothing but watch.

As Chak-Rah and Orenda moved to the edge of the mist, she turned to the man who had blown the substance into Nazshoni's face. She held out a knife for the man, and he walked, somewhat rigidly, over to the deer woman and took the knife.

"Kill her," Chak-Rah said and then turned and led Orenda into the darkness. As she passed the multitude of black-eyed men, they turned and followed her.

Nazshoni struggled to move as the man with the knife stepped toward her. She glanced over and could barely see Kanuna, who also lay with eyes open, staring blankly into the night sky.

The man hovered over the woman warrior. She believed his frightening eyes staring down at her would be the last thing she would see.

He raised the knife, and just as he was about to plunge it into her heart, several of the young warriors jumped onto him and, with a tremendous effort, managed to hold him down, while another of the young warriors pushed a piece of cloth into his mouth.

The black-eyed man struggled fiercely as Nazshoni watched, still unable to move. While the young warriors kept the man secure and quiet, Chief Mulimo came and investigated the darkness as if to be sure Chak-Rah did not hear the commotion and return.

He then turned to Nazshoni. After looking her over, he motioned to someone that Nazshoni could not see. Several women then came.

"Quickly, take her away from here. Hide her. We'll stand watch to ensure Chak-Rah does not return for her."

With this command, three women picked Nazshoni up and carried her to a dimly lit hut, then lay her on a sleeping mat and covered her with a light cloth.

Slowly, Nazshoni was able to move her tongue and lips.

"Kaaahunna... Kahnuunaa?"

One of the women came to her while the other two peeked out the covering of the door.

"What?" she asked, seeming puzzled by Nazshoni.

"Kaahnuuna... Oonnzi?"

The woman nodded, seeming to realize what Nazshoni was asking her.

"Your brother and Onsi?"

Nazshoni nodded, just barely, and was able to move her hand enough to take hold of the woman's arm.

"I think they're all right. The chief and some of the young men are taking care of them." The woman then glanced nervously to the doorway.

Soon, Nazshoni was trying to stand. Against the women's pleas, she stumbled out the door and toward the place they had slept, falling to the ground several times.

The morning sun was beginning to light the village as she came to Chief Mulimo.

"Where's my brother? Where's Onsi?"

The chief had been watching the direction that Chak-Rah had disappeared in but came over to Nazshoni.

"You should rest. It's not safe. Chak-Rah wants you dead. We waited as long as we could before it was necessary to intervene, but she could return when she realizes her slave has not come back with her."

"Where are they!" Nazshoni shouted.

Kanuna then stepped out of the hut where they had been assigned to sleep. He was rubbing his head.

Nazshoni immediately ran to him, embraced and held him as if he were a young boy of nine or ten.

She then stepped back and looked him over, still holding his arms.

"Where's Onsi?"

"He's inside, still having some trouble moving. What was that stuff?"

The two then looked over to the man who had been ordered to kill Nazshoni. He had been tied up and now writhed about as if he were an animal in a trap. He made a frightening growling sound as he twisted in his bonds.

A woman was standing a few feet from him, watching with tears in her eyes.

"Is there anything we can do for him? Can we remove the eye coverings?" Nazshoni asked.

The chief came over to them.

"No. We've captured Chak-Rah's slaves before. If we remove the eye coverings, the man will go completely mad. The woman there, she is the man's wife. She knows it will only be a matter of time before he dies unless we release him back to Chak-Rah. He will not eat or drink while bound."

Nazshoni left Kanuna's side and went into the hut. She came out with her bow and quiver of arrows.

"Where is Chak-Rah? Take me to her. I'll kill her today."

As she slung the quiver of arrows to her back, Mulimo attempted to calm her.

"Please, you must wait. If you charge into her lair, you'll be killed for certain."

"WHERE IS SHE? SHE HAS MY HUSBAND!" Nazshoni shouted, causing all those around her to step back in fear. Even the chief appeared to tremble slightly with Nazshoni's obvious resolve.

"I... I'm not sure where she is," Mulimo answered meekly.

Nazshoni's face twisted in anger. "You're not sure? You said you could find her!"

"Yes...we can find her. She always resides in a cloak of blood-colored mist. But you should consider your actions. She's very powerful. You will be killed if you try to take her now." The chief paused and then continued.

"You cannot ride in and kill everyone in sight. Many of her slaves are men of this village. They are husbands and fathers."

Nazshoni began to pace around the camp area. Those watching her thought she might burst at any time as she seemed to barely contain herself.

"We'll need to gather all that can ride. And ropes... we'll need as many as we can gather. We'll tie her slaves up. I'll kill her myself!"

As she said this, seemingly to herself as much as anyone around her, the chief stepped closer.

"I'll not send our young men into danger. We've tried a large attack before, and it failed. We have no more men to spare."

After he said this, one of the young men, who was perhaps fourteen or fifteen, stepped closer.

"We can help. We're not afraid."

Chief Mulimo turned quickly to the young man.

"No! You will not enter Chak-Rah's lair! You must help protect what is left of our people. I'll not squander you on a hopeless cause."

"But she is Nazshoni. She is a great warrior," the young man replied.

"Yes, and where is Orenda, the Storm Rider, at this very moment?"

The young man's face twisted a bit and his head lowered with his chief's question.

"Show me where she is. I'll kill her myself. Just show me where she is!" the bowwoman said, still in an obvious state of rage.

Kanuna came to his sister just as Onsi stepped out from the hut, seeming dazed by the effects of the glowing dust.

"Perhaps we should consider what the best manner of doing that would be. It will also give Onsi a chance to clear his head," Kanuna suggested with a soft voice.

Nazshoni grimaced, then stated with a firm voice, "We'll plan quickly and leave at noon." She then moved to where the horses were kept.

Kanuna glanced at the chief, and both expressed a loss about what to do.

The three warriors prepared their gear as the sun moved to the midday sky. Five of the young village men came to Nazshoni; they also carried weapons and ropes.

"Your chief doesn't want you near Chak-Rah. Just show us where she is. We'll do the fighting."

The eldest of the group replied to Nazshoni as she was securing her horse's saddle.

"We'll find her for you. We know the area where she has stayed. And, if we get attacked, we'll have ropes and weapons, just in case."

The bowwoman expressed uncertainty but checked the saddle to be sure it was secure.

Nazshoni then turned and, leaning down, pulled a knife from her right moccasin boot. She examined it briefly, as if to be certain of its sharpness, then placed it back in her boot and mounted her horse.

Glancing down at the young man, she replied with anger in her voice, "You show me where she is. That's all I need."

As the others also mounted, Nazshoni called to Onsi and Kanuna, "Once we find her, we'll go in fast. You two keep the slaves busy; I'll kill Chak-Rah."

Kanuna and Onsi both nodded, and with this, they moved out of the village.

The eldest of the young men rode to the front of the group. Along the way, Onsi noticed several deer heads with blackened eyes. He cringed as they seemed to be watching him.

After around twenty minutes of riding southwest, the one leading slowed. Nazshoni rode up beside him as he came to a stop.

In the distance, they could see an odd, blood-colored mist laying across the ground.

"She's not far. She resides in the mist," the young man said.

"You can go back. We'll find her from here," Nazshoni told him.

The young man thought about this as the woman warrior slowly moved ahead.

"We'll follow along a bit farther to be sure this isn't a mist she's laid to confuse us."

Nazshoni glanced back and studied the young man briefly, seeming to give it some thought.

"Very well, but once we are sure she's in there, take the others back," she finally replied.

The young man nodded, and Nazshoni took the lead, with Kanuna and Onsi following close behind.

As they proceeded, the red mist became thicker. The plants and trees within the haze were either dead or dying. Soon, the strange vapor floated all about them in patches that were dense in some areas and thin in others, seeming to cling around trees and bushes.

Nazshoni turned back to the young men.

"You can return to your village. I sense Chak-Rah is here...somewhere."

The eldest of the young men glanced to the others. He turned and nodded to Nazshoni. She then urged her mount forward.

Chapter Five:

INTO THE CRIMSON MIST

Onsi and Kanuna followed the woman warrior, unaware that the five young men never turned toward the village. They glanced at each other, but since the eldest didn't turn and leave, the others stayed as well, watching as the warriors disappeared into the red haze.

For several minutes, the warriors rode cautiously forward. There were no sounds to be heard.

"So much for riding in fast," Kanuna finally said as they strained to see ahead of them.

Just as his sister was about to reply, several of the black-eyed men jumped from the mist. All three horses became spooked and reared up. Onsi fell from his horse. Nazshoni and Kanuna's horses took off, galloping in different directions, with their riders barely remaining mounted.

Nazshoni reined her horse in and finally managed to calm it. She then turned and quickly headed back in the direction she had come from.

Onsi found himself alone and quickly being surrounded by the black-eyed men. They moved closer as he turned from one to the other. Standing up, he held his tomahawk in a ready position.

Farther behind, the young men from the village heard something ahead in the mist. The leader squinted to see anything through the thick fog.

All five were startled a few seconds later when Onsi's horse came straight toward them out of the vapor at a full gallop. Several had to move their mounts quickly to avoid a collision with the panicked horse.

Once Onsi's horse had galloped past, the five young men looked at each other. Then, without a word spoken, the eldest turned his horse and spurred it into the mist, and the other four quickly followed behind.

Meanwhile, after a jostling ride into the misty woodlands, Kanuna also managed to calm his mount. He got the horse stopped and then turned to head back where he had last seen his sister and Onsi.

Just as the young warrior was ready to move, a large deer sprung from the mist and jumped up over the horse, knocking Kanuna from his mount.

After landing hard on the ground, the warrior looked around and spotted the deer. It was a strange sight; the animal, obviously a female, had a rack of antlers, just as a male would have.

The deer stood tall and ominous as it stared at him. Realizing this must be Chak-Rah, Kanuna glanced at his horse and the tomahawks hanging from his gear.

As soon as he began to stand, the horse walked slowly in a direction away from the young warrior. Kanuna whistled very lightly, almost under his breath, to stop his mount, yet the horse continued to slowly walk away as if being ushered by an unseen force.

The deer woman turned her head, which positioned the deadly antlers toward Kanuna. He stood all the way up and moved to get the weapons from his horse, but the horse moved away again. Chak-Rah charged with her sharp antlers pointed toward the warrior's chest.

Just as Chak-Rah was about to slam into Kanuna, he fell backward to avoid being impaled by the antlers. The deer woman then bounced up and over him as he fell to the ground.

Kanuna turned around, and as he located Chak-Rah, a red mist enveloped her. As the vapor cleared, Chak-Rah was a woman. Kanuna was immediately impressed with her beauty, and Chak-Rah smiled seductively, seeming to be aware of his thoughts.

As this was occurring, a multitude of the black-eyed men began to close in around Kanuna. Chak-Rah turned and walked away, disappearing into the woodlands and the odd red mist.

Having no weapon, Kanuna stood and prepared to defend himself with his bare hands. But this was futile as the black-eyed men raised what looked to be hollowed bones. As Kanuna turned to make a defense, the men blew on the hollowed bones, and glowing dust enveloped him. He inhaled and immediately became unable to move. The young warrior fell to the ground like a stone, and when the dust settled, the black-eyed men came and carried him away.

Far from Kanuna, Onsi made a break from the black-eyed men that were closing in around him. As they raised their long, hollowed bones, he darted through a gap and moved quickly into the woodlands.

As he ran, the mist became thicker. He looked back to see if the black-eyed men were behind him. With a thud, he slammed violently into a large tree and fell back onto the ground unconscious.

In the distance, Nazshoni galloped into the thickening fog. She went farther and farther, past the point she thought Onsi and Kanuna must have been.

She turned her horse again and went back. Still, there was no sign of her brother or Onsi. She called out, "Kanuna!" Her voice fell flat in the red mist.

Becoming frightened by the turn of events that had separated her from Kanuna and Onsi, she spurred her horse again. This way and that, she continued to search in vain.

Though Nazshoni already held her bow in one hand, she now pulled an arrow from her quiver and placed it in a ready position in her bow.

The woman warrior began to realize she had become completely lost in the mist.

She called out, "Kanuna... Onsi!" Once again, her words fell flat in the dense vapor. She searched in vain for both or either one.

Far from Nazshoni, Onsi woke up. He wasn't sure how long he had laid on the ground. His vision was blurred, and his head throbbed.

As he gazed up into the blood-red mist, a large deer stepped directly over him. He was startled by the beast as it looked down upon him. He tried to focus his eyes.

It was a female deer but had antlers like a male would have. It turned its head in a human fashion as if studying Onsi.

The young warrior sat up a bit and moved backward to get away from the strange creature.

A red mist enveloped the large deer, and as the vapor cleared, a beautiful woman appeared. She had a headpiece made from the antlers of a male deer. Even with the odd headpiece, she was one of the most beautiful women Onsi had ever seen.

The woman walked slowly over to Onsi. He felt he should get up and run, but fleeing from a beautiful woman also seemed strange and cowardly.

As the woman came very close to him, he realized this must be Chak-Rah, but thought he could perhaps talk to her and avoid a confrontation.

She knelt to him and smiled. Her eyes gleamed.

As Onsi began to speak, she raised her hand, the palm facing upward. She then gently blew into the palm of her hand. A fine glowing dust wafted into Onsi's face, and he immediately became petrified.

Meanwhile, Nazshoni desperately tried to escape her entanglement with the mist. She could find no way to get her baring. The light from the sun filtered through the haze, but she could not determine its location in the sky.

The silence became almost unbearable as only the sounds of her horse's movements could be heard.

Nazshoni slowed her mount. As she peered into the mist, movement caused her to instantly raise her bow and arrow to a ready position.

In the distance, she could barely make out a large animal. Though not for certain what kind of animal, she immediately let her arrow fly. The mist became thick. The bowwoman placed another arrow in a ready position and moved toward the beast she had shot at.

When she arrived at the place the animal should have been, there was nothing to be found.

Again, silence prevailed. For what seemed an hour, she cautiously moved through the silent haze. She would hear or see something ahead of her. She would ready her bow and arrow but could not be certain of her target.

As she slowly lowered her bow once again, she noticed movement to the right and quickly turned with her bow aimed and ready to let the arrow loose toward the potential threat.

She found her arrow pointed at a large, horned owl, sitting perched in a tree. It looked down to Nazshoni as she lowered her bow and ushered her horse forward.

Again, she moved about, searching for her enemy or her brother and Onsi.

Then, as she rode through a dense area of mist, three of the black-eyed men stepped quickly from behind trees and bushes. They held up hollowed-out bones that were straight and around the length of her forearm.

The men spooked her horse, yet she maintained control. Just as she was about to turn her mount, the men blew into the hollow bones, and the glowing dust went all around her and the horse. Nazshoni immediately held her breath, but the horse fell, petrified underneath her.

Struggling to free herself from the downed animal, she scrambled away before inhaling any of the glowing dust. When she had gained some distance, she took in a much-needed breath of air.

Quickly, she readied her bow and arrow. Now, all around her, she heard noises in the mist. She turned from one noise to the other, hoping to identify and get a shot at Chak-Rah.

From behind her came the sound of footsteps. Turning with her bow and arrow, she saw another black-eyed man moving rapidly toward her. He held one of the hollowed bones in his hands, and it was obvious he planned to blow the glowing dust into Nazshoni's face and cause her to become petrified.

The bowwoman almost let her arrow fly, but she knew well this man was merely a slave to Chak-Rah. He was a son or father to someone in the village. Nazshoni began to back away as fast as she could to avoid the glowing dust.

She turned to run, and from her side, she caught a glimpse of something. Just as she looked in that direction, a large deer with deadly antlers came rushing toward her.

The woman warrior barely had time to drop her bow and arrow to grab the antlers with her hands and prevent becoming impaled by them. Even so, the sharp points scratched and penetrated the skin in several places as Nazshoni suddenly found herself being shoved through the woods by the beast.

As she slid down, still holding the antlers and now being drug across the rough ground, Nazshoni looked into the deer's eyes and immediately realized this to be Chak-Rah.

The weight of the bowwoman was pulling Chak-Rah's head down as she pushed Nazshoni through the woods. A split second later, Nazshoni slipped under the deer woman and was battered by hooves. Yet, as she continued to hold onto the antlers, they were pulled down and suddenly driven into the ground. Nazshoni became trampled again, and as the deer woman stumbled, she let go.

Chak-Rah flipped head over hooves and fell hard onto the ground. Nazshoni had been battered by the confrontation, and her buckskin clothes were tattered and torn. Blood ran down from several gashes and wounds. Yet she stood and faced the deer woman.

As Chak-Rah recovered and regained her footing, Nazshoni scanned the ground. Spotting a tree branch, she picked it up and charged toward her enemy.

Chak-Rah had not quite recovered from the hash fall and barely had time to turn her antlers to deflect the blow of Nazshoni's makeshift club.

The strike from Nazshoni staggered Chak-Rah, but the tree branch was half rotten, and it came apart after landing against Chak-Rah's antlers.

Now the bowwoman scrambled backward as the deer woman charged her, head facing downward.

Nazshoni fell away and rolled to avoid the deadly antlers, but Chak-Rah turned and reared up to trample the bowwoman with her hooves.

Raising her hands, Nazshoni caught the hooves before they could strike her face, but the back of her hands slammed into her left eye and cheek, causing a painful blow to her face as well as the back of her hand.

Again, Chak-Rah reared up and attempted to trample Nazshoni, seeming to target the bowwoman's face.

Once again, Nazshoni barely had time to deflect the powerful hooves with her hands. Once again, her own hands struck her face, lessening the damage that would have been inflicted by the hooves, yet Nazshoni felt as if she had been struck in the face by a strong man, as the back of her hand connected to her nose and lower forehead.

Quickly latching onto one of Chak-Rah's front legs, Nazshoni caused the deer woman to stumble and fall to the ground, then she staggered a few feet away.

As the woman warrior attempted to stand, a blood-red mist enveloped Chak-Rah.

The deer became a woman, and she looked identical to Nazshoni, except the woman wore the antler headdress.

Nazshoni held her side as pain racked her body, and she could barely get to her feet due to the beating she had endured. She could feel her left eye beginning to swell, and blood ran from her nose as she stared at Chak-Rah.

Then, the deer woman spoke, and Nazshoni was once again startled to hear her own voice coming from Chak-Rah.

"You will lose. Orenda is mine now. You must surely see that it's hopeless."

Nazshoni glanced around, trying to spot anything that could help her. Then she replied, more to gain some time than from a desire to talk with Chak-Rah. Her voice quivered from the agony that wrenched her entire being.

"You may have him under your spell, but you will never have his heart or his love. You have many men who serve you, but none love you."

Chak-Rah's face twisted in anger. The blood-red mist enveloped her, and suddenly, Nazshoni found the large deer bursting from it and charging straight toward her.

The bowwoman tried once again to grab the antlers. But, this time, Chak-Rah turned her head and antlers at the last second, perhaps wanting to avoid another tumble.

Nazshoni grasped the right antler with her right hand and held it tightly. She again found herself being violently drug through the woodlands, ripping her already ragged clothes even more. Struggling to hang on, the rough terrain scratched and tore at her battered body.

Knowing Chak-Rah would turn and impale her if she let go, the bowwoman searched for a way out.

A few seconds later, she was pulled along the edge of a ravine. She let go and rolled, then tumbled violently down it, causing more bruises and cuts.

Finally, she stopped rolling, and with all the strength she could muster, crawled to a bush, then pulled some dead leaves and branches over herself. She lay silent as she heard the sound of Chak-Rah moving back around and down into the ravine.

As the deer woman moved about, searching the area, Nazshoni suddenly felt more alone than she had ever felt before. Perhaps Chak-Rah was right. Perhaps it was hopeless. A tear erupted from her eye and rolled down the side of her face.

It was growing dark before Chak-Rah gave up. Nazshoni finally relaxed some and fell asleep under the leaves and brush.

Chapter Six:

ESCAPE OF THE FORLORN

As sunlight broke through the trees the following morning, Nazshoni moaned in pain. She felt as if a bear had mangled her and then tossed her over the side of a cliff. She could barely move without her entire body crying out in agony.

Cautiously, she half-crawled and half-stumbled away from the area, still fearing Chak-Rah would be close by, searching for her.

Her left eye was so swollen she could barely see anything from it and had to turn her head in awkward directions to see from her right eye.

Finally, after traveling a long distance in what she thought to be moving toward the small village, she came to a creek. Falling beside it, she pulled water up to her mouth and drank again and again.

The water revived her some. She could see it was close to noon but also realized she was unsure where she was or where to find the village.

Struggling to her feet, she again moved in the direction she thought the village to be. Even in her battered condition, she knew well it would be her only hope for survival.

It grew hot as the day moved toward afternoon. Nazshoni struggled to continue. Every step was painful, and now hunger began to torment her as well.

Later, the sun began to set. As she stumbled around lost, and in a daze, the woman warrior suddenly found herself in front of a black-eyed deer head tied to a tree.

Fear gripped her very being as she knew well these were the eyes of Chak-Rah. She began to move away from it as fast as she could. Several times, she fell to the ground.

Night slowly took over, and she could go no farther. Finding a large bush, she crawled under it and attempted to get as comfortable as she could. Weary from her wounds and hunger, she finally fell into an uneasy sleep.

In the middle of the night, sounds not far away from her startled Nazshoni awake.

Opening her one good eye, she turned her head toward the noises and spotted torches moving about. Again, terror clenched her heart. She tried to breathe as quietly as possible, yet her wounds and dire condition made it difficult.

Slowly, the torches moved closer. As they came into view, she could see three of Chak-Rah's black-eyed servants leaned over, walking to and fro as if searching for something. Nazshoni had little doubt they were looking for her. She had tried to get far away from the deer head but knew she'd not gone far enough.

Back and forth, Chak-Rah's slaves moved. They came closer, and Nazshoni felt certain they would hear her labored breathing. Several tears rolled down her face, yet she remained frozen, enduring the agony of her situation.

Finally, after what seemed hours, the black-eyed men moved farther and farther away until she could no longer see the torches. After shifting her body to ease the pain, she again fell asleep.

Morning dew chilled Nazshoni's body when she woke. She felt as though she had no strength to crawl from under the bush. The sun rose into the sky, and still, she could not find the will to escape her hiding spot.

As the day crept close to noon, the woman warrior realized she must get out or surely die under the leafy plant. With much pain and mustering all the resolve she could, Nazshoni pulled herself from under the bush.

Standing, she confronted the reality of not knowing where she was. She stumbled forward and barely avoided falling onto her knees and laying back down.

Step by step, she moved onward. Her head hung down as she was too weary to hold it up. She walked aimlessly now, simply trying not to stop and fall to her knees. She watched the ground as one foot moved past the other, knowing now she was completely lost.

The sun moved to an afternoon sky; still, the bowwoman moved forward, refusing to collapse and die. Her only goal now was to continue moving.

Then, as her blurred vision could barely make out the ground in front of her, she noticed something. It was a trail. She opened her one good eye as wide as she could and examined the find. The pathway had obviously not been used much, but it was something. Immediately, her spirits rose slightly.

After a difficult decision of which way to go, she began moving along the old path. Step by step, again, she forced her legs to keep moving.

As the day was turning to evening, Nazshoni arrived at the small village. Several elderly women stood as she staggered into the area.

When Nazshoni was sure the women had seen her, she fell to her knees and then flat onto her face, completely spent.

For several days Nazshoni floated in and out of consciousness. She would wake slightly as women cleaned her wounds and fed her a type of soup. Then she would drift back to sleep.

Finally, in the middle of the night, the bowwoman woke with a clear mind. As she lay on the mat, staring at what looked to be the top of a cave, she remembered the events that had brought her to this point.

Sitting up, she almost shouted, "Kanuna!"

A woman came to her, "Sshhh," She then glanced out the small cave opening into the darkness.

The swelling in Nazshoni's left eye had gone down some, and she could see from both of her eyes. She looked around as the woman attempted to calm her.

"Where am I? I've got to go. I've got to get my brother.... My husband, where is my husband? And Onsi?"

"Ssshhh," the woman said and once again glanced with apprehension out the opening, then replied, "You are the only one to return. We've not seen any of the others."

The woman warrior struggled to pull air into her lungs. She could barely breathe and felt she might pass out.

She looked around at her surroundings. There was only a dim light from a small fire. She examined the cave as her heart beat rapidly. She thought it might explode in her chest. The thought of losing all those she loved tore at her very core.

"I've got to go. I've got to help them," she said in a hushed voice.

"You must rest. You must calm yourself. Chak-Rah has been searching for you. We brought you here to keep you safe, but you must stay calm. Your life is in danger."

The words of the village woman did little to calm Nazshoni. Feeling completely helpless, she began to weep. After what seemed many hours, the sun began to rise.

As the bowwoman sat in the cave, staring at the dying fire, Chief Mulimo came in and sat down across from her.

"It's good to see you're awake. We weren't sure you would live."

Nazshoni glanced at the chief and then back to the fire. After a few seconds of thought, she replied.

"Perhaps I should have died. I've lost everything. I don't know how to regain what I've lost. But I want to make her pay, even if it takes my last breath."

The chief studied her for a moment. Then spoke softly.

"Chak-Rah has been searching for you. We didn't know what her slaves were looking for until you returned to the village. But after your return, we realized her servants have been searching for you, night after night. It seems she wants very much to destroy you. Perhaps you did more damage in your battle with her than you realize."

The woman warrior looked at him. Her battered face expressed no emotion.

"I don't believe that I laid a single scratch on her. She has stronger magic than I've ever witnessed."

Both thought about this for a few seconds, then the chief asked, "Can you tell us anything about the five young men who escorted you to Chak-Rah's lair?"

Nazshoni expressed confusion.

"They were told to return to the village. Did they not do so?"

The chief shook his head no.

"Only Onsi's horse returned. It seems you and the horse are the only ones that made it out."

Nazshoni turned back to the barely smoldering fire. Her face dropped in despair. Then she thought of something and perked up a bit.

"What about the old shaman at the edge of your territory? Perhaps he can help."

Now Chief Mulimo expressed confusion.

"Old shaman? I don't know of an old shaman at the edge of our territory."

The bowwoman studied the chief. She then turned back to the smoldering embers of the fire. Her face became stern in thought.

"An old shaman spoke to us before we came to your village." She paused and then continued while staring at the dying fire. "Perhaps it wasn't a shaman, but Chak-Rah... Either way, it seems I need to talk with him again."

"But what if it is Chak-Rah? She may kill you as soon as you arrive," the old chief replied.

"Perhaps...but, if it's not Chak-Rah, he may be the only one who can help us. Maybe he has some magic that can assist us. He said she destroyed his village, and he has been following her to avenge his people. If that's true, he could be on our side."

The two considered this. Then the chief said:

"You should heal before you go. And when you do, you must avoid Chak-Rah's eyes, which are all around."

Nazshoni quickly replied, "There's no time for me to heal. My husband, my brother, and Onsi are all I have. I'll go today...." She paused, then went on. "But you are right about her eyes. I will avoid them."

Chief Mulimo expressed sadness. "You were close to death when you returned to our village. If there is any hope of defeating Chak-Rah, you must recover first."

Nazshoni looked at him. Her left eye was still swollen, though she could open it enough to see him. She looked back at the fire and replied, "I cannot wait and heal while those I love are in danger. Anger runs through my veins. It will give me the strength to keep going."

Struggling to stand, then limping with pain, Nazshoni followed the chief out of the cave. After a lengthy walk, they arrived back at the village.

Chapter Seven:

SECRETS OF ORENDA

The woman warrior ate a meal, got cleaned up and changed, then packed a few supplies and weapons on Onsi's horse. As the sun moved into an afternoon sky, Nazshoni struggled in pain but managed to mount the horse and left the village.

Being careful to avoid the black-eyed deer heads, she made her way to the old shaman's camp. As the sun was setting on the horizon, Nazshoni found the site and dismounted her horse.

There seemed to be no one around. The large rock sat vacant in front of the rough lean-to. The woman warrior tied her horse to a low tree branch and then walked around, searching for the shaman.

Several minutes later, he walked from the woods, wearing the cougar pelt and carrying an armload of firewood.

"Hello," he said and then went straight to the fire pit in front of the lean-to. He put the collection of broken branches and limbs down beside the pit and then glanced at Nazshoni.

Noticing her bruised and battered appearance, he winced slightly, then, sitting down, picked up a stick, and began to stir the embers of the fire.

Nazshoni watched him closely but cautiously sat down on the opposite side of the small pit.

Soon, the fire began to take hold again, and the old shaman tossed a small branch into it.

As the light of day gave way to night and the light of the flames flickered around the small campsite, the old shaman moved in a manner to become more comfortable, then began to speak.

"Perhaps...I should have put more effort in my warning of Chak-Rah."

Nazshoni quickly replied, "Perhaps you are Chak-Rah. Maybe I should seize the opportunity to kill you now."

The old shaman briefly thought about this.

"Perhaps you should. But if you are wrong, then you will have killed an innocent person and destroyed any assistance I may possibly be in your struggle against her."

The bowwoman expressed no emotion but continued to stare at him with suspicion in her eyes.

The old shaman again stirred the small fire. Then Nazshoni asked:

"What does she want with Orenda? Why did she take him? How can I destroy her?"

After taking in a deep breath, the shaman replied.

"Why does she take any man? She uses their living essence to strengthen her own existence. As for your husband, I'm not certain why she took him. I would need to know more about him—that is, beyond the stories, which may or may not be true."

The shaman gazed into the fire for a few brief seconds, then continued.

"I know the name Orenda means 'high spirit.' To my knowledge, it's not a name given often at birth. Though I have known shamans that have changed their name to Orenda, it was later in life. What is Orenda's birth-given name?"

Nazshoni gritted her teeth.

"The secrets of Orenda are not given freely. Will you help me fight Chak-Rah?"

The shaman had been poking a stick into the fire but raised his head to look at Nazshoni.

"No," he said.

"Then I'll tell you nothing," the woman warrior replied, with wrath in her voice.

"I didn't say that I wouldn't help you. But I'll not fight Chak-Rah...again. I've faced her in battle before and nearly lost my life. Her dark magic is too strong for me."

"Then why do you pursue her? What is your purpose, if not to destroy her?"

The old man again studied the fire as he considered his reply. After more poking with the stick, which caused embers to dance into the night air, he spoke.

"There is very little hope of defeating Chak-Rah in battle. I pursue her in the hope that an edge will be found someday, or that she will let down her guard for some reason, or that a warrior such as you might inflict enough damage to weaken her. Then I might have a chance to stop her. But, from your wounds, it seems that has not happened."

Nazshoni's face became slightly relaxed, and she looked down at the fire. Both sat quietly for several long moments.

"If I tell you the things you wish to know, do you promise you will help me?" she asked.

He examined her battered face and again expressed compassion, then looked back at the fire and replied.

"I don't know that anything I can tell you will be helpful. But, if I understand Orenda better, I can be more certain about what she wants with him. Though I have my suspicions, there are several possibilities. I would like to be sure what I tell you is accurate and something that might give you an edge or something that will give you some understanding. That is all I can promise. If I knew of a certain thing that would give someone an advantage, I would have used it already."

The woman warrior studied the elderly man. Her head then lowered to the fire, which crackled and splashed light across the two weary faces.

After several long minutes, Nazshoni began to speak.

"Orenda is the son of a great warrior chief. He has never told me his birth-given name. He said that person died with his family.

"When Orenda was very young, his father began to train him as a warrior. When he was a teenager, the great Chief Tecumseh began to gather tribes together. He spoke of an Indian confederation, which would be large enough to negotiate successfully with the white man and, if need be, to defend itself from the white man.

"Orenda's father moved their tribe closer to Tecumseh and became an advisor to the chief. Orenda spent many hours in the company of his father and Tecumseh as they discussed the future of the confederation.

"When Orenda was around sixteen years old, his father was called upon by Tenskwatawa, who was Tecumseh's brother. The messenger explained that a large military force of white men had arrived at the edge of the confederation's territory. Tecumseh had gone west to meet with other tribes and would not be back soon."

Nazshoni became quiet for a few seconds. She took in a deep breath as the old shaman watched her. Then she continued.

"Orenda's father went to gather his warriors together, with Orenda following. His father told him to stay, but Orenda asked his father if he considered him a child or a woman. This made his father change his mind, and Orenda, with his two tomahawks, went to fight with the other men of his tribe.

"It was a terrible battle. The white men have called it the 'Battle of Tippecanoe,' though I have heard other names as well.

"Young Orenda fought bravely by his father's side. Yet, the father was struck down before his son's eyes by the musket ball of a white soldier.

"It was at this time that Orenda said he lost his spirit as a man. He became like an animal with uncontrolled rage. He began to strike down the white soldiers without restraint and became covered from head to toe with the blood of his opponents.

"He fought until he collapsed on the battlefield, exhausted. There, he stared at the smoke-filled sky as the soldiers pushed Tenskwatawa's forces back.

"He was empty and sickened by the death of his father and the death he had inflicted. He no longer felt like a man but more as a beast.

"Later, he managed to stand and escape into the woods. He went as quickly as he could to his home. But the soldiers had already passed through, killing and burning. He found his family slaughtered and laying on the ground.

"Orenda was able to move his family's bodies into the woods and bury them, but then had to leave quickly as the white soldiers began to pass back through on their return from the battle.

"After this, he wandered aimlessly for several weeks. He came across a small group of people who were fleeing more soldiers. They gave him some food and explained the soldiers were demon-possessed. They had a lust for killing and had deserted the white man's army to kill and obtain treasures from the Indians.

"Orenda paid little attention to the stories as he ate. He was dead inside. He cared about nothing or no one. He huddled around a small fire with an empty mind and spirit.

"Later, the group began to move again, and Orenda walked along with them, as he had no place else to go. He held a buckskin wrap over his body and stared at the ground as he walked.

"Then, to their rear, a young warrior rode up quickly from the direction they had traveled. He had been shot and fell from his horse as others gathered around to help him,

"As Orenda came close, he heard the warrior say the demon soldiers were approaching rapidly from behind. The warrior then died.

"The people became panicked and began to run. Suddenly, twelve white soldiers rode into the group and herded them together. Several tried to escape the soldiers, and they were immediately shot down.

"Orenda stood watching. The soldiers jumped down from their horses as women and children wept. One of the soldiers demanded all the teenage women be brought to them. He then began looking through the people's belongings.

"As one elderly woman refused to give her possessions to another soldier, he pulled his pistol and shot her down. The loud shot caused Orenda to step back. He looked at the dead woman, but still, he was empty of anything.

"Then, another soldier pulled a young woman from the group. She screamed, and the soldier hit her in the face, which caused her to fall to the ground.

"At this time, an elderly woman turned to the people. She was weeping. She looked at all of them and asked, 'Is there even one here who will defend the helpless?'

"Orenda said it was like lightning striking his heart. It took a few seconds to surge throughout his mind and spirit, but suddenly everything became clear. He suddenly realized who he was. He was no one, and yet he was the one person who could defend these helpless people.

"The soldiers had become focused on raping the young woman when Orenda attacked. He struck like a mountain lion. With his tomahawk, he struck down one of the soldiers, then very quickly took a musket from another one.

"With one blow, he took that soldier down with his own musket, then shot another as he moved toward Orenda. Dropping the musket, he grabbed another soldier and pulled him in front of his own body to take the musket ball of another demon soldier. Immediately afterward, he pulled the pistol from the dead soldier's belt and shot the man who had just killed his own comrade.

"One by one, he killed all twelve within a few minutes. He then stood in the middle of these dead, demon soldiers."

Again, Nazshoni paused. She seemed to be recalling the tale.

The old shaman picked up another piece of wood and placed it on the fire. He then looked at the woman warrior, and she continued.

"The people stood in awe of what had just happened. Then, the woman who had asked if there were anyone to defend the helpless said, 'Orenda,' meaning one with a high spirit. Then, others began to say it as well.

"From that time on, he became Orenda. That was when the legend was born.

"He stayed with the group for a while but then began to wander. The story of his defeat of the demon soldiers had already spread like fire.

"Everywhere he traveled, there seemed to be helpless people in need of defense. As he fought to defend the weak and helpless, they, in turn, proclaimed him a hero of the oppressed.

"Even my brother, Kanuna, and I would sit as children and listen to stories of his battles. To believe he would one day be my husband was more than any young girl could have dreamed.

"When I was sixteen and Kanuna was fifteen, our small village was almost completely wiped out by a band of rogue warriors seeking weapons and horses. They took a small group of teenagers, which they planned to sell to the slavers. My brother and I were among those who would have been sold.

"Orenda came across the murderous warriors before we reached the slavers. He pretended to trade a musket for Kanuna and me, but he knew the murderers would try to kill him. Once they attacked, he destroyed them very quickly.

"I didn't know he was Orenda at the time, but I think when he saved us, I fell in love with him.

"Only by persistence from Kanuna and myself did he finally allow us to travel with him and eventually began to train us as warriors. Orenda and I were married not long after I turned eighteen. Two days after our marriage, we were allied with a tribe that was battling Blood Hawk and his four hundred warriors."

Nazshoni looked up at the old shaman. He sat considering her tale for several minutes as the fire crackled and more embers danced into the air.

Then he looked at the bowwoman and began to speak.

"So, one man died in battle, and a new man was born in battle. The warrior Orenda and the purpose of his higher spirit came together in one instant of inspiration."

The old shaman returned his gaze to the fire as Nazshoni watched and listened closely.

"The words that stir a man's spirit are very powerful. Perhaps the words that inspired once could do so again."

Silence returned to the small campsite. The shaman poked the fire as he gazed into it. Then he went on.

"You love Orenda, but do you love him enough to die for him?"

Nazshoni thought about this and replied.

"You say there is little hope against Chak-Rah. I've already faced her once and failed. I will not leave my husband and brother or our companion Onsi. I will fight until they are free, or I am dead. So, yes, I will die for him."

The old shaman continued.

"Love is perhaps the only thing that can defeat Chak-Rah. It could break the spell on Orenda. Perhaps, if there is a shred of love in Chak-Rah's heart, it could even stop her. Love is a very powerful tool if it is wielded in its true nature and at a time when it would be most effective.

"Orenda risks his life to defend the helpless. It seems he would or may someday die defending the weak." He then looked at Nazshoni and asked, "Would you let him die for the helpless if that was what needs to happen?"

Nazshoni's face twisted in fear and anger.

"What are you talking about, old man? What are you asking?"

He looked back to the fire and replied.

"I now feel I know what Chak-Rah wants from Orenda. Though darkened with anger and a lust for power, Chak-Rah has a high spirit as well. It runs strong in her bloodline. I feel she wants to have offspring from him. She will then raise them in the dark arts. They will be powerful, and she can create her own dark tribe of slaves and servants."

The woman warrior appeared to have trouble breathing. She tried to respond, though obviously distraught.

"She wants to have children...by my husband?"

"Yes, but she will transform herself to look like you. While Orenda is under her spell, he will believe it is you."

Nazshoni broke in, "She's already done that. I watched her transform herself to look and sound like me."

Seeming a bit surprised, he glanced up at her and replied, "If that's so, I'm even more certain about it. I suspect she needs to kill you first. You are the only danger to her plans right now. She would also wish to have a marriage ceremony under the full moon. It would strengthen her spell over Orenda.

"There will be a full moon in a few days. If her plan is successful, many people will suffer for years to come.

"She'll remain close to Orenda to protect her prize. She'll have her slaves search for you.

"However, if you are very careful, you may be able to get close enough for one shot before she becomes aware of your presence. I don't believe you will be able to kill Chak-Rah. But you could be certain she is not able to produce the offspring she desires."

Nazshoni's face became even more stretched with fear. Her head began to shake back and forth.

"No.... No, you can't ask me to do such a thing. I...could never do such a thing." As she said this, a tear welled up and rolled down her cheek.

The old shaman stirred the fire with his stick. He then continued.

"I had a dream of the future; it was long before you and your husband arrived here. The dream was not clear, but there was one thing in it that I understood for certain. A man with a high spirit must die to stop Chak-Rah."

Nazshoni again replied, "No... No... I don't care about your dream! There must be another way!"

"What would Orenda say?" The shaman asked.

The bowwoman stared into the fire. Another tear rolled down her cheek. She shook her head again.

"That's the help you have for me? To suggest I kill my own husband?" she finally asked.

He stood and, looking down to her, replied, "Did you expect a magic arrow?" He then walked over to the lean-to and laid down on a thin mat.

The following morning, the old shaman sat up. He looked over to the smoldering fire and saw Nazshoni sitting cross-legged, staring at the dying embers.

Walking over to the side of his lean-to, the old shaman picked something up. He then moved over to Nazshoni.

"I don't have any magic arrows, but I did find this in the woods the other day. Maybe it will help you."

Glancing up, Nazshoni saw that he was holding her bow.

"My bow.... I lost it while fighting Chak-Rah." She then stood, took the bow, and looked it over.

"So, it's your bow? Well, that's even better. It has found its rightful owner."

The woman warrior looked at the old shaman. Seeming reluctant to talk, she finally replied.

"Thank you for returning my bow."

The elderly man expressed compassion and replied, "You're welcome. I'm sorry the situation is so dark. Chak-Rah has done much damage to many villages. Your loved ones are far from the first to fall prey to her. I'm not a warrior, I would not be able to help you in the battle you must fight, but I hold out hope that she will be stopped."

After eating a light meal with the shaman, Nazshoni carefully made her way back to the village.

When she rode into the small community, all the villagers began to gather around her. She dismounted and walked the horse to the hut they used for storing their gear.

Chief Mulimo came up to her as she finished securing Onsi's horse.

"Did you find the shaman? Will he help you fight Chak-Rah? What did he say?" The chief asked with much concern in his voice.

Nazshoni looked at him, and then she looked across all the faces of the young boys, old men, women, and children who watched her with hope in their eyes.

"I found the shaman. He won't help me fight Chak-Rah. He said there's little hope in fighting her."

Immediately, the faces of the villagers dropped with despair. Nazshoni turned her attention to the horse and began to undo the saddle.

The chief looked at the villagers, which still stood watching him and Nazshoni.

"Well, what are you going to do?" he asked.

The bowwoman stopped and looked at him, then the villagers, who also waited in anticipation of an answer. She didn't reply for several seconds as she thought of what to say to these heartbroken people. Finally, she answered.

"I will hope a little and fight a lot." She then went back to undoing the saddle.

Chief Mulimo's face expressed concern.

"The shaman said it was hopeless. You will certainly die if you fight her again."

Nazshoni again stopped her work with the saddle. She again considered her words briefly before replying.

"I would rather die trying to save the ones I love than live knowing I gave up." She then turned back to the saddle and, undoing the strap, pulled it from the horse.

The villagers looked at each other and then slowly began to walk away. The chief was the last to finally leave.

Chapter Eight:

THE LAST HOPE

After removing the saddle from Onsi's horse, Nazshoni went into the hut and pulled one of her fighting outfits from a pack. She then gathered some arrows together and found a spare quiver she had held onto.

Leaving the hut, she found a large hollowed and halved gourd used to carry water or grain. She then began to go from one dead fire to another. She would scrape the top of the ashes off until she found the black charcoal remnants.

As Nazshoni worked, the villagers remained in the distance and watched. The chief came to the group, and as they followed Nazshoni around the huts, they talked among each other.

When Nazshoni had the large gourd container almost full of black charcoal scraps, Chief Mulimo approached her.

As Nazshoni stood up from a fire pit, she noticed him. Behind the chief were around fifteen of the villagers: several boys who were not quite teenagers, older women, and men. They stood behind their chief and stared at Nazshoni.

The woman warrior's hands and forearms had become black from her labors with the charcoal. She rubbed some sweat from her forehead with the back of her arm, and it left a black streak on her brow.

She examined the chief and others but said nothing. Then the chief spoke.

"We have decided that we too would rather die trying to free our loved ones than live knowing we gave up."

The woman warrior quickly replied.

"You have children and elders to care for. You need to consider those who depend on you. I'll fight Chak-Rah."

Chief Mulimo said:

"The mothers, younger women, and a few of the older boys will stay behind with the children. If we're not successful, they will be instructed to take the children and leave this area forever."

Nazshoni said nothing for several seconds. Then a slight smile crossed her face.

"We'll need some clay, also rope, rags, and scraps of buckskin."

After she said this, the villagers smiled and immediately began searching for the items she had asked for.

The remainder of the day was spent preparing for the next confrontation with Chak-Rah. Nazshoni took some of the clay the villagers brought her and began mixing it with water. When the texture was right, she began to blend it with the charcoal. Soon, she had a black liquid the density of a thick broth.

Nazshoni poured the mixture into a large, hollowed log, which the women used for washing clothes. She then took the buckskin outfit she had pulled from her pack and, placing it in the black mixture, dipped it several times until it was completely covered. Then she took it to a nearby tree and hung the now black outfit up to dry.

Once the villagers realized the purpose of the black mixture, they continued to make more as others brought outfits and, using the thick liquid, blackened their outfits and hung them to dry as well.

Later, after the sun went down, Nazshoni went to the cave and slept. Chief Mulimo told her the black-eyed slaves of Chak-Rah had been searching the village during the night in an apparent effort to find the bowwoman.

The next morning, Nazshoni was up early, instructing the villagers and moving about to ensure everything was ready.

She again blended the charcoal and clay together with water. This time, however, she used more clay and less water. After much mixing, she had a black paint-like substance and covered the mixing container to keep it from drying.

As the sun lowered in an evening sky, they prepared themselves.

Nazshoni came from a hut dressed in her blackened outfit. The other villagers also began dressing in their blackened clothes.

After securing her long dark hair with a leather strip, Nazshoni began to apply the black substance to her face and any area of her body that might reflect light.

Soon, the woman warrior and the villagers were almost completely black.

They mounted their horses and, with packs in hand, cautiously rode toward Chak-Rah's lair.

After slow and careful maneuvering through the woodlands, they dismounted from the horses at the outer edge of the blood-red mist. By this time, the sun had almost set, and darkness was taking over the day.

Once the horses had been hidden and secured, the group began to make their way into the mist.

Soon, Nazshoni spotted one of the black-eyed men. He stood like a statue, staring into the twilight. Nazshoni motioned for several of the young men to follow her and the others to stay put.

Carefully, the woman warrior moved around behind the servant of Chak-Rah. Then, before he realized anything to be wrong, she had a rag around his eyes, and the others were pulling him to the ground.

One of the young men stuffed a piece of buckskin into the man's mouth to keep him quiet, and they quickly tied him up.

Noticing a long, hollowed bone and satchel hanging around the man's neck, Nazshoni took them and found the small satchel to be full of glowing dust.

"This should be helpful," she whispered, and the young men smiled. They then went back to the others.

Once again, the group crept through the mist and brush. In the distance, they spotted another of Chak-Rah's servants.

"I'll move around behind him. When you see me wave, make a noise, just enough to distract him." Nazshoni told the chief. Then she took the long bone and dipped it into the glowing dust. Checking the end, she saw a small amount had pushed into the tip.

Slowly, the woman warrior moved around and to the back of the black-eyed man. Finally, the chief noticed her wave, giving him the signal.

Taking the branch of a small bush, the chief moved it about, causing a soft bristling of the dead leaves. Soon, the servant of Chak-Rah turned his attention to the sound and began to move toward it.

At this time, Nazshoni moved up quickly behind him. She was bent down, and by the time the man noticed something toward his back, Nazshoni was crouched directly behind him.

When the man turned around, Nazshoni blew the dust up into his face, and he immediately became petrified as stone. He fell backward onto the ground, and the bowwoman quickly covered the black eyes with a cloth.

As the chief and villagers came to Nazshoni, they saw she was removing this man's hollow bone and satchel of glowing dust.

Once they were gathered around, she handed the bone and satchel to a young man, who was perhaps twelve years old.

"Do you think you can use this?" She asked him.

The young man examined the long, hollowed bone and then opened the satchel.

"Push the end into the dust," she instructed the young man. He did as she instructed.

"Now, when you're ready, blow the dust into your opponent's face. Like this." She then put her bone to her mouth and pretended to blow.

The young man raised the hollow bone to his mouth, but rather than pretending to blow on the bone, he inhaled a breath with the bone to his lips. Sucking in the dust, he immediately became petrified and fell back.

Nazshoni expressed dismay, then turned to one of the elderly women.

"Stay with him," she told her. The bowwoman pulled the long bone and satchel from the young man's hands and gave it to an elderly man. He looked to be in his sixties and not in great health, but Nazshoni had few options.

"Here. Don't do what he did," she told the man. Then she turned, and again the group moved farther into the red mist.

As they traveled into the fog, they encountered more of Chak-Rah's slaves, guarding the deer woman's lair. But Nazshoni and the villagers quickly developed a method for dealing with these sentries. With each black-eyed guard they overcame, they took his glowing dust and hollowed bone. Soon, all the villagers had a long hollow bone and a satchel of the dust.

After several hours of careful movement, the group could see a radiating area in front of them. It was as if the mist was on fire.

Nazshoni crept closer and closer. Sweat rolled down the side of her head, but she remained focused on the strange luminous area facing her.

Noticing shadows through the mist, Nazshoni took the bow from across her back. She then pulled an arrow from her quiver and placed it in a ready position in the bow.

Approaching a flat field with only a few dead trees, she could finally see Chak-Rah standing among several large fires burning around the area. The deer woman had her back to Nazshoni and, standing at a table, appeared to be working on some type of magic potion or powder. The large table, made of log halves, also held a variety of plants and herb-related materials.

The bowwoman crept closer.

Unexpectedly, as Chak-Rah moved to the side to pick up ingredients, Nazshoni became shocked by the sight of Orenda. A chill ran down the back of her neck and across her spine.

The warrior was standing with his back to a large, dead tree. His hands, arms, and lower body were intertwined with vines and roots to hold him secure and in place. His eyes were covered with black clay, and white eyes were painted over the black substance. He stood petrified like a statue, spellbound and unaware of anything around him.

Nazshoni's eyes welled up with moisture as she lifted her bow and arrow. A tear rolled gently down her cheek as she took aim at her husband.

The arrow was pointed straight to Orenda's heart. Another tear rolled down from her other eye. She began to tremble. An involuntary mummer erupted from her lips.

With the arrow ready to take flight, Nazshoni suddenly moved it from Orenda to Chak-Rah. She let the arrow fly.

Chak-Rah became like a mist just as the arrow was about to hit. It flew through the mist, and as it hit a tree on the far side of the field, Chak-Rah could be seen, as a large deer, turning and charging toward Nazshoni.

The bowwoman stood and pulled another arrow from her quiver. She placed it in her bow but didn't have time to pull it back. Chak-Rah was too close.

Suddenly, from the mist, black-eyed men emerged all around them. The villagers now stood and attempted to hold the mass of Chak-Rah's slaves back.

Nazshoni fell away from the charging deer woman and barely escaped the sharp antlers.

As she stood back up, the bowwoman noticed the villagers and Chak-Rah's slaves both falling to the glowing dust, as villager and slave alike used it on each other.

She quickly turned back to Chak-Rah and saw the deer woman was again charging her.

Though she didn't have time to use her bow, Nazshoni still held the arrow. As the deer woman closed in, Nazshoni stepped away and then plunged the arrow into the dear woman's side. This caused Chak-Rah to change form, and as she did, she avoided the arrow but fell and rolled as a woman.

Now, Nazshoni dropped her bow and charged. Before Chak-Rah could change form again, the bowwoman had leaped on top of her. She plunged the arrow down toward Chak-Rah's heart, but the deer woman caught her arm and held the arrow away from her chest.

Chak-Rah rolled, and Nazshoni found herself in a wrestling battle with the deer woman, struggling to keep away from the sharp antler headpiece as Chak-Rah tried again and again to gouge her. The deer woman's eyes expressed a stern resolution to destroy Nazshoni.

Back and forth, they twisted and rolled, both fighting for the arrow and a possible edge over the other.

Then, Chak-Rah pushed Nazshoni away from her, and before the woman warrior could get another hold on her, Chak-Rah transformed into the large deer.

Nazshoni realized Chak-Rah was not able to change form while in contact with another being. She maneuvered herself to avoid the charging deer, but as she did this, she felt that she must find a way to limit Chak-Rah's ability to change forms...somehow.

As Nazshoni avoided the antlers from Chak-Rah, she moved toward the large fires to see the battleground better. Yet, it was very difficult not to look at her husband, who seemed oblivious to the life or death struggle a few short yards away.

The red mist was illuminated by the fires and presented a surreal vision as the bowwoman again avoided a charge by Chak-Rah. The battle became focused in the open area around the deer woman's large table and the fires.

Nazshoni found a large stick on the ground. It looked to have been fashioned as a club-like weapon, perhaps used by the black-eyed slaves of Chak-Rah. Tossing the arrow aside, she quickly prepared for the next attack by the deer woman.

When Chak-Rah came close, the woman warrior stepped aside and swung the large club, connecting with the antlers and causing the deer woman to stagger back. But she quickly charged again, this time rearing up and using her hooves to strike at Nazshoni.

The bowwoman swung at the dear woman's legs but missed. Chak-Rah then landed two painful hoof blows into Nazshoni's shoulder and chest area, causing her to fall back onto the ground.

She struggled to catch her breath and barely had time to roll away from another attack by Chak-Rah. Though she escaped the deadly hooves, Chak-Rah turned her antlers and sliced across Nazshoni's back as the bowwoman scrambled to escape.

Nazshoni screamed out from the pain and lost her hold on the club.

Still struggling to breathe, the bowwoman scrambled away, then staggered to her feet. She could barely remain standing, and as she gazed over to Chak-Rah, the deer woman transformed back into her human form. Stepping over to the club, which lay on the ground, she glanced down at it, then over to Nazshoni.

"Did you really believe that you and a small group of villagers could defeat me?"

As Chak-Rah asked this, black-eyed men began to move from the mist. Nazshoni looked all around and realized she was surrounded by Chak-Rah's slaves, indicating all the villagers had been defeated.

Stepping back and closer to her husband, Nazshoni called out, "Orenda... Orenda...please wake up. Please...help me."

Chak-Rah laughed under her breath.

"He's mine now. You'll die. Orenda and I will have many beautiful children. We'll rule this land for many, many years.... We'll be happy."

Nazshoni looked around at the black-eyed men as they stood staring at the woman warrior. Gaining her breath back but still unable to straighten up from the wound on her back, Nazshoni replied defiantly, "All you have is a slave. I have a husband."

This angered Chak-Rah. Her face twisted, and a frown developed across her mouth. But she remained where she stood.

Nazshoni took several deep breaths, turned slightly away from Chak-Rah, and then moved her hand down to the knife in her moccasin boot. As she took hold of the handle, she set her legs.

"For that, you will die slowly and painfully," Chak-Rah said.

Nazshoni continued in her struggle to breathe. But after a few seconds, she replied.

"Pain has always been a companion of mine. It would be strange not to have the old acquaintance by my side when I die." The bowwoman then carefully slid the knife from her boot but still held it beside her leg to avoid revealing the blade to Chak-Rah.

The deer woman's face again expressed wrath.

At this instant, Nazshoni summoned all the strength she had left and charged Chak-Rah.

Raising the knife, she jumped the last few feet. Chak-Rah's eyes widened with surprise. But just as Nazshoni was about to strike the blade into the deer woman, she became like mist, and the woman warrior passed through it and landed on the hard ground, rolling several times before coming to a stop.

Turning, she staggered to her feet, attempting to hold the knife up in a defensive position.

As quick as lightning, Chak-Rah had changed into a deer and was upon her. She struck the hand holding the knife with her antlers. The weapon flew from Nazshoni's grasp and fell into the ground, blade first. Stumbling backward, Nazshoni looked over at the weapon now stuck into the earth, handle up.

Holding her wounded hand, she felt she would pass out at any second. Then, to her dismay, Chak-Rah charged her. Nazshoni held up her hands in defense, but Chak-Rah raised onto her hind legs and, using her front hooves, landed two quick blows into Nazshoni's chest.

The woman warrior stumbled backward and landed hard against a tree. She then slid down to a sitting position.

Struggling to get air into her lungs, the bowwoman had no strength left to stand.

Chak-Rah transformed into her human form. She looked over to Nazshoni and smiled victoriously.

For several long seconds, there was only an eerie quiet. Then, from the shadowy mist, Kanuna walked toward Nazshoni. His eyes were blackened, and the false white eyes were painted over the dark clay substance.

Nazshoni began to weep.

"Kanuna... Kanuna, please...help me." She coughed and tried to move, but the pain was overwhelming. Tears streamed down her eyes, leaving traces in the black charcoal paint.

Her brother knelt to her as Chak-Rah watched on, still smiling.

"Please...help me, Kanuna." Her voice was almost a whisper of agony as black-eyed Kanuna stared briefly at her from a foot away.

Then, he lifted his hand and opening it, palm facing the sky. He blew the glowing substance into Nazshoni's face. She immediately became petrified as a stone.

Chak-Rah laughed under her breath again as Kanuna stood and slowly walked away. When the deer woman stopped laughing, a strange calm settled over the battleground.

The fires crackled, and the red mist continued to glow. Nazshoni gazed around and saw many black-eyed men staring with blank, painted eyes toward the battle area. They stood like statues looking toward Chak-Rah.

As the bowwoman labored to bring air into her lungs, Chak-Rah walked over to Nazshoni's knife. She reached down and pulled it from the ground.

"Now, you'll die by your own blade," Chak-Rah said as she started moving toward the petrified bowwoman.

Then, to Chak-Rah's side, Nazshoni saw a large, horned owl fly into a tree overlooking the open field. It looked down toward Chak-Rah.

Suddenly, to Nazshoni's amazement, the owl flew down from the tree, and while in flight, it transformed into a large cougar. The cougar landed on Chak-Rah and let out a blood-curdling scream as it pinned the deer woman to the ground.

Chak-Rah was shocked as she landed hard onto the dirt. With Chak-Rah pinned to the ground, the large cougar again growled at the deer woman, showing its large teeth.

With one swing, Chak-Rah embedded Nazshoni's knife into the chest of the cougar. The cat let out another scream—this time, one of agony.

Chak-Rah pushed the beast from on top of her, and it immediately transformed into a man. It was the old shaman they had first spoken with, the same one who had returned Nazshoni's bow.

Leaning over on one arm, with the knife in his chest, he looked up to Chak-Rah.

The deer woman's face twisted with shock; she let out a cry of anguish. "Father... No... No." She then moved over and gently took him into her arms.

"My daughter...if there is any love in your heart left for me, I beg you...please turn from the darkness."

Chak-Rah began to shake her head in disbelief. She began to cry.

"Father... No... No."

The old shaman then lifted his hand gently to his daughter's cheek. Caressing it softly, he said, "I love you." Then his head fell back.

Chak-Rah began to weep without restraint. She rocked her father and cried out, "No, Father... No... No."

A few minutes later, a blood-red mist enveloped her and her father. It glowed brightly for a few seconds, then the mist, Chak-Rah, and her father were gone.

Nazshoni still struggled to breathe, but after seeing Chak-Rah disappear, she passed out.

When she woke, the morning light was flowing in through the trees. The red mist was gone, and Chief Mulimo was looking at her with concern in his eyes.

"Are you all right?" he asked. "We thought you had been killed."

Nazshoni sat up a little, and her entire body screamed with pain. Her face grimaced as she attempted to get onto her feet.

With much effort and help from the chief, the bowwoman stood and looked around. All the black-eyed men were in the same places they had been before. The people of the village appeared dazed, seeming to have also recently overcome the petrifying effects of Chak-Rah's dust.

"You defeated her? You defeated Chak-Rah?" the chief asked as the bowwoman tried to walk.

"No, I didn't defeat her." She replied, seeming to labor for every breath.

She wearily lifted her head and looked over to Orenda.

"Then, where is she?" he asked as he assisted her.

Struggling to take one step after another, she replied with an exhausted voice.

"I don't know. She was about to kill me. But the old shaman... He was her father and a shapeshifter too. He became a cougar and saved me. But she stabbed him. I... I think he realized it was the only thing that might stop her. I think he sacrificed himself...hoping she would lose her lust for power."

She limped closer to Orenda, who remained as all the other black-eyed men, petrified and standing like a statue.

Smoke from the now dying fires drifted about as the woman warrior came face to face with her husband. She looked at him and then touched his face with her bloodied and battered hand.

"Perhaps he stopped her. But it didn't break the spell on her servants. My heart is full of sadness for these men. What will become of them?" As the chief said this, he looked around at the many servants of Chak-Rah.

Nazshoni gave no reply. She simply stared at Orenda.

Mulimo then walked over to some of the other villagers, leaving Nazshoni alone with her spellbound husband.

"I love you," Nazshoni said softly. Orenda's white-painted eyes continued to stare blankly out into the morning light.

Nazshoni laid her head upon his chest and began to weep. She rubbed his arm as her tears fell onto his upper body.

"I love you.... I love you so much." Her voice cracked from pain and despair. "I can't live without you." She looked up to him again. Still, he did not move.

The woman warrior sniffed and wiped a tear from her eye. She then looked down at the ground as she held her husband. Her face strained as she considered the harsh situation.

Then, her eyes widened a bit. Seeming to remember something, she looked back to her husband.

Speaking with a soft voice, she asked, "Is there even one here who will defend the helpless?"

For a brief second, nothing happened. Then Orenda jerked slightly. Nazshoni stepped back and watched closely.

Orenda's arm moved. Then his other arm moved. Nazshoni put her hands to her mouth and began to cry again.

The black clay-like substance around Orenda's eyes began to crack. He began to move his legs but was still bound by the roots and vines.

Suddenly, he raised his right hand, pulling it free from the vines, and then began to feel his eyes. He started clawing the black substance from them.

As he did this, his left arm began to move and broke free from the bonds.

As soon as he had his eyes cleared enough to see, Nazshoni stepped forward and wrapped her arms around him, weeping with joy.

Orenda put his arms around her but gazed about in confusion.

As Nazshoni held onto her husband, she heard shouts of joy.

Looking around, she saw that all the black-eyed men were coming out of their trances. Their fellow villagers and loved ones were gathered around them as they pulled the black clay away from their eyes.

The woman warrior laughed as tears rolled down her cheeks. Then she began to slide down to the ground. Her eyes rolled to the back of her head, and she fell back onto the hard earth.

Chapter Nine:

THE HEART OF VALOR

The following day, Orenda, Kanuna, and Onsi stood staring down at Nazshoni's motionless body. She lay in a bed, her arms to her sides. Bruises on her face and arms distorted the appearance of the beautiful woman they knew. Cuts scattered across her skin relayed the fierce battle she had fought as they examined her with sadness.

Onsi turned away from the other two as a tear escaped and rolled down his cheek. He quickly wiped it away, then glanced back at Orenda and Kanuna as if to be sure they hadn't seen it.

Orenda took in a deep breath. Then, he straightened up and strained to see in the dim light of the mud hut. Noticing Nazshoni's eyes open slightly, he rushed over to her side.

Gently taking her battered hand in his, he knelt to her.

With a soft, raspy voice, she asked, "Did we win?"

Several tears welled up and almost erupted from Orenda's eyes. He smiled and nodded, "Yes, my love. We won."

Nazshoni smiled and drifted back to sleep.

Slowly, the woman warrior's condition improved. Orenda, Kanuna, and Onsi hovered over her as a mother hen would a chick.

A few months later, Orenda walked in from brisk fall weather outside the hut. He was confronted by Nazshoni chastising Kanuna.

"I can eat by myself!" She then turned to Orenda.

"Husband, will you please tell my brother, for the last time, I can eat by myself! I'm not a helpless child!" She then glanced over to Kanuna, who still held a plate of food.

The warrior looked at Kanuna and then to his wife.

"Well, we should look at those wounds again before making any hasty decisions."

Nazshoni's face expressed shock. Orenda turned to Kanuna and winked. His brother-in-law turned away from Nazshoni and smiled slyly.

"We should look at those bruises on your chest first," Orenda said as he came close to her.

Nazshoni backed up a bit as her husband reached up and, pulling her buckskin dress out, peered down at her chest.

"Hmmm," he said.

The woman warrior reached up and pulled her dress from his fingers, closing it back up.

"What do the bruises on my chest have to do with anything?" she protested.

"We must be sure you're mending well. You are, after all, the only bowwoman in the group."

His wife looked up to him with a puzzled expression.

Orenda then reached down and, taking her buckskin dress, began lifting it up.

"Now, let's look at those wounds on your back."

When he had lifted the dress up above her knees, she took hold of his hands, stopping him.

"You want to look at my back? What does my back have to do with me being able to feed myself?"

Orenda gave her a look of compassion.

"It's because we care about you," he said, never losing his solemn expression.

Nazshoni searched his face, seeming very unsure about the entire situation.

Kanuna had turned away when Orenda began lifting his sister's dress. But now, he was heard trying to restrain a laugh.

Nazshoni's expression immediately changed to anger. She glanced over to Kanuna, and then pulling her dress away from her husband by stepping back, she slapped him on the chest.

"Get out of here! Both of you!" she said rather loudly.

With this statement, Kanuna lost it and began to laugh aloud. Orenda also chuckled and smiled. They both began to move toward the small doorway.

"Leave the food!" she demanded, and Kanuna sat it down before exiting behind his brother-in-law.

Once the two were out, Nazshoni picked up the plate of food. She examined the dish briefly and then smiled brightly to herself.

The four stayed the winter in the small village. They were treated like family by the villagers and were welcomed to stay forever. But the warriors knew their destiny lay west.

The woodlands were searched again and again for any sign of Chak-Rah. There would be no sight of her ever again, though several of the warriors told of hearing a woman weeping in the thick of the forest. When they ventured toward the sounds, the weeping would always fade away.

The following spring, Orenda approached Onsi, who sat with many children gathered around him, all wide-eyed and mouths agape.

Onsi was concluding the story of the lofa. He had told them the tale many times over the winter. Orenda stopped and listened.

"And that's how the terrible lofa were defeated, and our village was saved."

A hush fell over the gathering. The young boys and girls then smiled with delight.

The warrior smiled slightly as well and continued toward Onsi.

As he came closer, the children stood and gathered around, examining the scars on his arm, just as they had done many times before.

"Can I speak with Onsi, children?"

The children smiled, and a few laughed with joy as they trotted away.

"We'll be leaving soon," Orenda said. Then turned and looked back at the children, now in the distance.

"Don't they ever get tired of hearing that story?" he asked.

"Well...it's not actually their favorite."

Orenda looked at him with an odd expression of disbelief. Then Onsi began to smile.

"Their favorite is the story of Nazshoni and her battle with Chak-Rah, the deer woman. They never tire of that one."

Orenda smiled and patted him on the back as they turned and walked toward their horses.

"Now that one is my favorite as well," the warrior replied.

The End

TWELVE MINUTES
TILL MIDNIGHT

Gray Door Ltd.

THE DAYS OF RECKONING

A swarm of cicadas filled the warm day of May 1934 with their chorus of screeching songs. Suddenly, the insects halted their long chirps and an eerie silence overtook the dusty Louisiana road.

After a moment of the unnatural quiet, a man of around forty, in well-worn clothes and holding a ragged coat in his arm, stood up from beside the road.

He was common in appearance yet stood tall and held an air of dignity about himself, even in his weathered apparel.

He moved slowly to the road's edge and stood watching down the long stretch of gravel.

Soon, a dark colored Ford sedan came traveling toward him at a rapid pace. The car came into view with a contrail of dust billowing behind.

As soon as the sedan passed by the man, brakes were applied, causing the car to slide a bit and come to a noisy halt about twenty yards past him.

The man beside the road turned, and as if anticipating the arrival of a car, began walking through the dust toward it.

As he came closer, a sweaty young man got out of the front passenger door and walked to the back of the car. He opened the rear driver's side door and looked back down the road to where the man now stood.

"I'm riding back here." The young man said in a rough voice and then climbed into the back seat.

The man walked around to the passenger side of the car and seeing a woman laying in the back seat, he opened the front passenger door.

The driver also appeared rough and had sweat beads on his forehead.

A musk smell mixed with cigarettes and whiskey resonated inside the interior of the automobile.

Once the doors shut, the young man in the back said, "Let's go Henry," and the driver took off quickly, causing the tires to spin rocks and dust into the air behind them.

Warm air entered the car through the open windows and allowed a small amount of reprieve from the humid Louisiana heat.

Henry was a young man in his early twenties. He appeared nervous as he drove the Ford sedan, glancing toward the man with suspicion in his eyes.

The passenger now noticed that Henry had a pistol sitting between his legs. The edgy young driver looked over toward him again and then glanced at the rearview mirror on the passenger door.

He began to speak in a low, aggressive voice. "Don't be getting any ideas." He again glanced at both side mirrors, as if someone might come up quickly behind them. Then he checked the rearview mirror and continued in the same tone.

"You know that's Bonnie and Clyde back there don't you?"

The passenger glanced back at the two people in the back. They appeared tired and uncomfortable. They seemed to be sleeping or trying to sleep. The passenger turned back to the driver.

"I was just catching a ride. Maybe I should be getting out now." He said politely with a southern drawl.

Henry smirked at this. He again checked the mirrors as the car juggled around from the rough gravel roads. "There ain't anyone getting out now, unless Clyde says so. Or we all die in a hail of bullets."

The passenger again glanced at the pistol between the driver's legs before he turned to the front windshield.

Suddenly a large bug connected violently against the windshield directly in front of him, causing him to flinch. Henry chuckled a little at this. The passenger turned to Henry and watched him a few seconds. He then turned his attention to the scenery passing by outside his window.

After almost an hour of driving, they pulled down a side road. There stood the remnants of a house. From what could be seen, a fire likely destroyed the home and after years of abandonment only fragments of the original structure could be seen.

Henry and the passenger climbed out and began to stretch a little. Clyde exited the rear door of the car and quickly limped around to the other door. He opened this one and carefully assisted Bonnie out. She appeared to have a wounded leg. She limped with Clyde's help to a stump and laid against it.

Clyde pulled two cigarettes from a pack in his pocket. He quickly lit both and handed Bonnie one. She immediately began to pull drags from the cigarette, as if desperate for the nicotine, and then blew the smoke out quickly so she could pull another drag from it. The grayish blue smoke briefly floated around her before disappearing.

After watching this, the older man that was picked up from the roadside found some brick remains of a porch support and sat down facing the two, while Henry scanned the area in a manner to detect any unseen threats.

Clyde retrieved a few things from the back seat of the car and then the trunk. He tucked a pistol under his belt, and placed several bottles of whiskey on a flat area close to Bonnie.

"Go see if you can get some gas, and cigarettes; maybe something to eat too." Clyde sounded winded as he told Henry this.

Henry nodded and left quickly in the car.

Clyde placed a folded jacket behind Bonnie and gave her a drink from a whiskey bottle. She coughed a little after taking a drink. When she coughed, she grimaced in pain and held her leg. She lay back on the stump and closed her eyes.

The afternoon waned. Clyde began to move about, gathering pieces of wood and placing them into a pile. The man watched Clyde with apprehension but said nothing. The outlaw in turn continued to glance over at the man from time to time.

The man was older than Clyde. He could see Clyde must be in his early to mid-twenties. Yet the young man appeared tired and spent. After several tense moments of watching each other the older man spoke.

"I don't believe I belong here. I'll be moving along."

Clyde sneered at the man. "You may not belong here, but you're here now. You got a problem with the company you keep?"

The older man said nothing but picked up a stick and raked it on the ground in a drawing fashion.

Clyde continued. "You don't look so important to me. What good are you? All the good folks out there that don't want anything to do with Bonnie and me; they all got some occupation they pride themselves highly of. So what is it you're good for?"

The man casually dropped the stick and gazed at the ground when Clyde asked him this. He then folded his ragged coat and repositioned it over his leg in a manner suggesting he wouldn't be leaving soon. After a few seconds he replied to Clyde, but without much zeal.

"I've done some writing over the years. But folks haven't been reading my work much lately. Now days I just seem to wander around here and there; sort of like the wind I suppose, speaking, where folks will have me; in churches and community buildings sometimes. But most folks seem to want someone to talk to rather than do any listening."

Clyde chuckled at this as he knelt down to light some scraps of paper under the small pile of wood.

"Yeah, times are tough all over ain't they? You sound like a preacher to me. That's what all those high and mighty preachers like to do, write stuff and then talk to people. Tell folks how bad they are and how they're all going to hell. Are you a preacher?"

The fire began to slowly blaze as Clyde asked the man this.

"No." The man said, almost in a whisper.

"Yeah, well, I think you're the same thing as a preacher whether you admit it or not."

Clyde blew lightly on the small fire after saying this. The fire became a little larger as he did.

Once the fire took hold and began to burn on its own Clyde stood back up. He walked over to Bonnie and checked on her. She lay asleep, though rustling about occasionally as if uncomfortable.

He then sat back down; staring at the small fire and glancing up at the man from time to time. The evening stressed toward night as the two men eyed each other.

Clyde flipped his cigarette into the fire and stood up. He moved over to the whiskey bottles and picked one up. He took a drink and wiped his mouth on his shirt sleeve. He pulled another cigarette out of the pack with his mouth as he stared across the fire at the man.

Once his cigarette had been lit and he'd taken a long drag from it, he spoke again as he exhaled the smoke and paced slowly around the fire.

"I've been wanting to tell someone the real truth of things. You look like someone that'll know the truth when you see it."

The young outlaw took another long drag and expelled it toward the sky. He thought for a second and then continued.

"You see Preacher, Bonnie and me; we're doing all the good people a favor, even though they don't seem to realize it. We're fighting all the corrupt government people and the bankers that take people's land. We should be heroes. The truth of the matter is the government trains people to go out and kill. And they say it's all right when soldiers do that for the government. But they call Bonnie and me 'murderers.'"

Clyde took another drag from the cigarette as Preacher watched from the other side of the fire. He spewed the smoke out quickly and continued. "And the government takes people's land. They steal good folk's land from them. They kick them off their own land and call that repossession for past due taxes. But they call Bonnie and me 'robbers.' So, you see Preacher, we're the good ones, cause we're fighting for all those folks out there that won't fight. That is the truth Preacher, that is the real truth."

Clyde took another drink of whiskey as if to stress his statement before he looked over at Preacher with interest.

Preacher sat silent. He gazed down at his feet and rubbed the worn toe of his shoe in the dirt. Clyde took another long drag from his cigarette and blew the smoke out as he gazed off into the evening sky.

Finally, Preacher looked up at Clyde and in a stern voice asked.

"Is that the truth Clyde? Is that the real truth?"

Clyde froze in place when Preacher asked him this. He turned and stared at Preacher with a slight anger in his eyes. He took another drag from his cigarette and appeared to consider Preacher's question briefly before replying.

"Everybody thinks they know all about the truth. Everyone has their opinion about the truth. But all those opinions are different. The truth is, Bonnie and me are just defending ourselves. I want everyone to know that. That's my truth Preacher. We're just defending ourselves from the law. We're just trying to survive. We're not bad. The law is the one that's bad. If the law would leave us alone there wouldn't be any reason to fight."

He then stared at Preacher in anticipation of an answer. He quickly lifted the bottle up for another drink. He wiped his mouth on his sleeve again then the sweat from his forehead.

Preacher used his forearms to lean on his legs. He gazed down at the ground between them as if searching for some hidden object. Darkness now took over and the fire began to create splashes of light around them.

As seconds passed by and the embers from the small fire danced high into the air, Clyde again glanced at Preacher. He smiled due to the long pause.

But then Preacher took a deep breath and replied with clear and unfaltering words. "You may speak what you consider to be the truth for you and Bonnie. But generally speaking, you're still wrong. And the general nature of that wrong defeats any truth you may hold on your own."

Now Clyde became animated and reacted to Preacher in anger.

"What is that? You tell me Preacher, why you think, what you just said, has anything to do with anything. No one can say what the truth is or isn't. If you know what the truth is then you tell me Preacher. You tell me right now what the truth of anything is."

Preacher never looked up as Clyde said this. Instead, he continued to scan the ground between his legs. But after Clyde finished making his statement Preacher casually looked up at him and replied calmly.

"I believe the truth is, every man knows right from wrong deep down inside. And this is a universal truth. Not the truth a person builds up around them by their own deeds. And every man and woman must face this truth in some form or fashion before they die."

Clyde stared at Preacher. He seemed surprised that he actually had an answer. Preacher in turn continued with his assessment after a brief pause.

"Whether people accept this, shall we say, 'spirit of truth' or not, doesn't change it Clyde. Whether a man allows himself to see truth or not won't eliminate its existence. But everyone will face the truth in some way. Each man and woman will have the opportunity to do the right thing. And this fact is one of those 'real truths' that no man will ever be able to alter by his own devices or actions."

Clyde continued to stare at Preacher with contempt. Then he turned to Bonnie. She was sitting up, staring into the fire. Clyde looked back at Preacher and sort of nodded at Bonnie, as if he'd woken her.

"How long have you been up Sugar?"

Bonnie moved a little and grimaced in pain as she did so. "Long enough," she replied flatly. "Give me a cigarette, would you?"

Clyde pulled a pack of cigarettes out and lit one. He handed it to Bonnie. Then he sat down beside her and pulled a cigarette out for himself.

Bonnie stared across the fire at Preacher. She pulled a drag from her cigarette and exhaled the smoke quickly.

Clyde handed her the whiskey bottle. She took a drink and her face twisted as she swallowed. Just as she put the cigarette into her mouth again a car could be heard turning down the lonely road.

Clyde stood and pulled the pistol from his belt. He stared with apprehension at the head lights rolling slowly toward them.

"It is Henry." He tucked the pistol back into his belt. Bonnie laid back as she could also see the familiar sedan moving closer.

Henry hopped out of the car, turning the headlights out as he did so.

"Anyone recognize you?" Clyde asked as Henry opened the back door of the car.

"I don't think so. I went to a small store on the edge of town that had just one old man working. He seemed too tired to care about anything."

Preacher noticed that Henry seemed to fear Clyde as much as respecting him. He was also obviously a little younger than Clyde. Preacher sat quietly and watched the unusual relationship with interest. Clyde treated Henry as an employee, but then also seemed to treat him as a grunt at times.

Henry pulled a sack from the back seat. He then pulled various food items and cigarettes out of the bag, setting them down with the items Clyde had beside the fire. As he stood back up Henry glanced over at Preacher. He said nothing to him and Preacher watched Henry with apprehension.

As Clyde and Bonnie began to eat, Henry went back to the car and retrieved another sack. This sack had several large bottles of whiskey and another bottle that Preacher couldn't tell for sure what the contents were.

They sat around the fire eating while Preacher watched. Then Clyde threw part of a loaf of bread over to Preacher.

After examining the loaf on the ground a few seconds, he reached down and gingerly picked it up. He then closed his eyes briefly. After a couple seconds he opened them up and began to eat the bread in small bites. As he did this, he glanced over to Clyde who now chuckled under his breath and sneered slightly at Preacher.

Later Clyde, Bonnie and Henry sat around the fire. They smoked cigarettes one after the other. They drank and played cards without stopping. Around midnight Preacher pulled his coat over himself and lay on the ground watching them until finally falling asleep.

The next morning, crackling embers of the dying fire greeted Preacher as he opened his eyes. Dampness persisted in the air. He sat up. The sun had not broken across the horizon yet. There sat Clyde across the smoldering fire, staring at Preacher with hollow, emotionless eyes.

Preacher looked at Bonnie and Henry as they lay asleep with thin blankets tossed over them. As he sat up, Preacher quickly turned his eyes back to Clyde and now refused to turn away or show weakness. Clyde in turn continued to sit stoically; examining Preacher in silence. The two remained in this state for several moments as the others slept.

When the light of the sun broke, causing a few rays to stream across Preacher's face, Clyde began to speak in a low voice. He struggled to sound friendly and more civilized than the previous night.

"All the good folks are saying Bonnie and I are killers and bad people. They should know we're just trying to defend ourselves from corrupt law people. Bonnie and I are fighting for all those good folks out there because they don't have the gumption to fight for themselves."

Clyde took a quick drag from his cigarette and continued as the smoke came from his mouth. "Someone like you could tell them our side of it and they would listen to you. If you told the people, we're out here fighting their fight, they might listen."

Preacher watched Clyde closely as he said this. Then he replied to Clyde after very little thought.

"I can't tell the people such a thing."

Clyde appeared puzzled by this answer. His voice became more hostile.

"You're supposed to be so good. You said yourself that you do speaking and writing. You said yourself you've attended churches. What do you mean you won't tell the people?"

Preacher picked up a small stone and tossed it into the remnants of the fire, causing tiny glowing embers to fly upwards. Then he replied as he watched the smoldering campfire.

"A man has a right to defend himself from an aggressor just as a country or even a town has the right to defend itself. It does this by asking a few of the citizens to fight the threat for the good of all the people. Are you defending yourself Clyde, or are you the aggressor?"

Preacher paused for a second as if in thought, and then continued.

"Unless the people asked you to fight for them, you ain't fighting for the people. You're fighting for yourself. Did any of those good folks you speak of ask you to do what you're doing?"

Clyde's mouth twisted with anger when Preacher said this. He took another drag from his cigarette and spewed the smoke out.

Just as Clyde was about to also spew a mouth full of curses out, Preacher turned to look at Bonnie. Clyde then also turned and looked at Bonnie. He realized she lay awake, gazing out across the dying fire.

"Give me a cigarette Clyde." She said with a weary voice.

Clyde pulled a cigarette from the pack and lit it for Bonnie. He handed the cigarette to her and she quickly began to pull a drag from it with urgency. He returned to his makeshift sitting spot and stared at Preacher with anger.

Preacher in turn watched Clyde with a quiet resolve. Occasionally he raked a small stick on the ground between his legs but otherwise didn't express weakness to the outlaw.

Soon Henry stirred and after a few bites of leftover food they all began to load into the car. Clyde assisted Bonnie into the back seat and with a flash of Clyde's pistol Preacher once again moved reluctantly to the front passenger seat.

As the car rumbled down the rough back roads Henry turned toward the passenger seat from time to time. Preacher glanced back at Henry but neither said anything. Bonnie smoked one cigarette after another.

Clyde continued to nurse a bottle of whiskey. He still seemed angry and when Preacher turned to look at him, he still had wrath in his eyes. Eventually Preacher simply watched the scenery go by.

Later in the afternoon they came close to a town. Clyde had Henry pull into a gas station and an attendant filled the car with gas.

Henry went inside and bought several more packs of cigarettes along with some sandwiches.

Preacher noticed Bonnie and Clyde sat in the back attempting to appear normal. They acted as if they were talking together in an effort to avoid revealing their faces to the attendant.

As the attendant washed the windshield he briefly stared straight at Preacher. And then he glanced back at Bonnie and Clyde as the two continued their charade of chatting together.

After the attendant finished with the windshield he moved around to the back of the car and this caused Bonnie and Clyde to relax some.

Preacher again glanced back at Clyde who checked out the back as the attendant continued his work. Clyde turned and looked at Preacher; then pulled his coat away from his waist to reveal his pistol. Preacher turned back to the front of the car and stared out.

After returning to the car, Henry started the sedan up and they drove quietly through the back streets of town. Once on the other side, the car picked up speed and soon they were far away. The Louisiana backwoods swallowed them up as Henry ventured onto familiar roads.

Then he turned down a narrow, seldom traveled road. The grass grew in the middle of this road and only the two-wheel tracks could be seen. Under the car the grass brushed the floorboards.

After traveling the primitive road about a half mile, Henry pulled off to the side of a creek and placed the car in a semi-hidden spot behind some small trees and brush. Then everyone wearily climbed out of the car.

A barren area, of around thirty feet, lay beside the creek. It was where the creek had risen and receded causing only rock and small stones to abide now.

"We'll stay here for a little while just in case anyone in town noticed us. Later we can get back on the road. We should still make it back to your Pa's place before dark."

After saying this Clyde helped Bonnie sit beside the car and immediately, she lit up a cigarette. Henry nodded in agreement and brought the sandwiches out. Then he pulled several large pieces of logs closer to sit on.

Preacher sat and watched them eat. Again, Clyde watched him closely as if waiting for him to ask for some food. Preacher said nothing, however. When they'd almost finished eating, Clyde reached into the paper bag and pulled out half a sandwich. He sat it on the log and then glanced over to

Preacher. He lit up a cigarette as Henry and Bonnie finished their meal. He smoked his cigarette slowly and continued to watch Preacher.

When Henry finished his meal, he stood and stretched. "I'm going to go keep watch." He then walked off toward the obscure road.

Clyde nodded. Seeing Bonnie had finished her sandwich he lit another cigarette and handed it to her. She climbed into the back seat of the car and sort of laid back in the seat as she smoked her cigarette.

When everything became quiet, Clyde took the half sandwich and walked over to Preacher. He sat the food down beside him. Then, he walked back over to where he was before and sat back down.

Preacher glanced down at the sandwich. He then looked back at Clyde who again watched him closely as he lit another cigarette from the one he'd just finished.

Several minutes passed by as the two observed each other. Then Preacher reached down to pick up the sandwich. When he did this Clyde straightened a little and took hold of the pistol handle in his belt. Preacher stopped before his hand touched the food beside him.

Clyde sneered a bit and then rubbed the handle of the pistol softly. Preacher slowly moved his hand to the sandwich without showing any emotion, but also never taking his eyes from Clyde.

Picking the food up, Preacher lowered his head a few seconds and then opened his eyes and placed his gaze immediately on Clyde again. He slowly took a bite of the sandwich and chewed with caution. Clyde chuckled and then moved his hand back from the pistol.

As Preacher slowly ate, Clyde reached over and picked up a near-empty bottle of whiskey. He turned the bottle up and finished about half of the remaining liquid in one large drink. Then he wiped his mouth on his sleeve, while grimacing from the taste of the alcohol. Once he'd recovered from the drink he again stared at Preacher.

"That's just like that couple we picked up a while back; all good, upstanding and law-abiding citizens. They didn't hesitate to eat food that was bought with stolen money though. All the good people suddenly turn bad when they get hungry."

Clyde paused briefly and then continued.

"You tell me Preacher, why isn't that the truth? You're eating food bought with stolen money. You talk to me about truth and then you eat a sandwich bought with money that was stolen from a bank. Go right ahead Preacher; tell me the truth about that."

After Clyde said this, he took another long drag from his cigarette. Again, he spewed the smoke out in a rapid exhale through gritted teeth and tight lips. He stared at Preacher and then stood up. He began to pace a little in front of the log.

Preacher finished chewing a bite and gazed at the sandwich, seeming to pay little attention to Clyde.

This pause caused Clyde to become more animated. Now he laughed under his breath as he stared down at Preacher. He turned the bottle up and took another drink leaving only a small amount in the bottle.

Preacher swallowed and without looking at Clyde, began to speak.

"When a soldier is taken prisoner, he doesn't turn down the food offered to him by his enemy simply because the food was grown on enemy soil. The bread did no evil. Nor does food commit crimes. I can give a piece of this bread to a bird and it won't poison the bird. And the bird won't question the origin of the offering either.

"The wrong occurred when you forcefully took the bounty of another man's labor. The fact that your prisoners eat food derived from evil gains won't undo the initial wrong committed. And it doesn't make them guilty of your crime."

Now Clyde's face contorted in a fit of anger. Preacher watched the flush of blood flow to his face, causing his features to express an immediate and evil desire to quench the rage welling up inside him.

Clyde immediately threw the whiskey bottle at Preacher just as a loud cry of violent intent burst from his lungs, "Aaarrhhhhgggggg!" Clyde's aim with the bottle was spot on. Preacher raised his arm just in time to deflect the projectile hurling toward him. The impact of the bottle caused a distinct clunking sound as it made contact, and then fell beside the log.

Preacher grabbed his arm in pain, but he never uttered a sound. He grimaced and held his wound as he kept his eyes on Clyde.

Now the pistol came quickly from behind the belt. Clyde aimed it straight toward Preacher's head.

"You're just asking for a bullet between the eyes Mister. I've shot men for no reason at all. Now you have the nerve to say such things to me. You just want a bullet to the brain, don't you?"

Preacher continued to stare at Clyde, as he rubbed his arm from the pain. Then he spoke but had no fear in his voice.

"You can try to destroy the truth, Clyde. You can shoot me and anyone else that speaks the truth, but that won't destroy it. The truth is all around us and inside us. You spoke the truth just now. You've shot men for no reason. That same truth is what convicts you of the murders, because no man in his right mind asks for a bullet between the eyes. You've lived by the gun and I suspect you'll die by it."

Clyde cocked the pistol slowly. His hand trembled slightly as he aimed squarely for Preacher's head. At almost the same instant that he pulled the trigger, Clyde moved his aim to the bottle beside Preacher. As the loud gunshot rang out, glass sprayed onto Preacher and around him.

From the back of the car Bonnie jerked up as the gunshot startled her from sleep. She looked out to Clyde and then shouted in a hostile voice.

"Clyde, would you stop doing that? I told you it makes my whole body hurt." She then lay back down with a sound of exasperation.

Henry came running up with his pistol pulled. He looked at the shattered bottle and then Clyde who still held the pistol in the air. Sweat rolled down the side of his head. He slowly put the pistol back into his belt. He sneered at Preacher and turned away from him.

"We should probably be going." Henry said meekly.

Clyde cursed under his breath and went to the back of the car. He opened up the door and nudged Bonnie to get her to move over.

With Henry behind him Preacher went to the passenger side and climbed in, still holding his arm.

Henry gathered everything and stuffed it into the trunk. He quickly checked on Bonnie and Clyde in the back seat, then scanned the area for anything incidentally left behind. The young outlaw moved to the driver's side and climbed in; he started the car and they moved back onto the road.

An hour passed with no one in the car uttering a word.

Then a car came toward them. Dust floated around the back of it as it hurled into view. Police lights on top could be seen and as they passed each other while a sheriff insignia revealed itself on the side.

Clyde checked out the back window until the threat had gone far behind them. "How much longer till we reach your Pa's?"

Henry glanced in the rear-view mirror, and then answered Clyde. "A couple hours maybe, it's taking longer on these back roads."

"Find another place to stop. We'll stay off the roads a while and get back on the way before dark."

Henry nodded and began watching for a suitable spot to get off the road.

Soon he pulled the sedan onto an old road. An abandoned house came into view as the afternoon sun lay around the ramshackle home.

Henry stopped the car behind some trees. The doors opened and everyone began to exit the car.

Clyde helped Bonnie over to an area of the porch that hadn't yet broken down. He gently helped her sit and quickly lit a cigarette for her.

Henry and Preacher watched by the car and from a distance. Then Henry leaned back on the hood of the car.

"We'll be at my Pa's house in a few hours." Henry said this as he continued to watch Bonnie and Clyde. "Maybe he can figure something out. You're pushing your luck; you know that don't you?" Henry turned his head slightly toward Preacher; who glanced at Henry and then turned back to Bonnie and Clyde.

"Yeah, maybe your Pa can think of something. But I'm not figuring I'll make it out of this alive anymore." Preacher said as he briefly looked back at Henry. After this he sat down on the running board of the Ford.

Henry lit a cigarette and spewed a cloud of smoke from his mouth.

Clyde walked over to the car. "I'm going for a walk. Keep an eye on Bonnie." He spoke to Henry and never glanced at Preacher. He then walked with a slight limp to the road and soon disappeared from sight.

Henry looked at Preacher as if he should move, so Preacher stood up and began walking over to where Bonnie sat. Henry moved behind him.

Bonnie sat leaning against one of the corner beams. Preacher sat across from her on the ground. Henry remained standing. He smoked his cigarette and looked around nervously. Bonnie flicked her cigarette butt past Preacher.

"Give me another cigarette Henry."

He pulled one from his pack and after lighting it, handed it to Bonnie. She quickly took a long drag from it causing the tip to burn brighter. As Bonnie smoked her cigarette she stared blankly at Preacher.

Henry paced around the area and began to examine the broken-down house as a slight breeze moved through. He walked to the side and investigated a broken window. Then he moved to the back.

"Come here." Bonnie said flatly to Preacher.

Preacher looked at her with some apprehension. He slowly stood up and with his tattered coat in hand, moved closer to her.

"Sit down. I'm sure not going to stand to talk to you."

He did as Bonnie said and sat on the ground in front of her.

She took another long drag from the cigarette. Blowing the smoke out in an apparent feminine fashion she stared at Preacher. Then she sat up a little more and leaned over on her knees toward him.

"You know, I've never seen a man stand up to Clyde before." She said this with a sultry voice.

Preacher looked at Bonnie with compassion in his eyes but gave no reply. After a few seconds Bonnie continued.

"If a man were to come along that could stand up to Clyde, I just might be inclined to get away from this." She pulled another drag from the cigarette and blew the smoke into Preacher's face in a flirty manner. Then she smiled and turned her head a little. She gazed out at Preacher from the corner of her eyes.

He lowered his head when she blew the smoke in his face. He then looked at Bonnie again as she gazed at him seductively.

"Yeah, I might go with such a man and start fresh. I might even go to work again. You know I got a lot of tips when I worked as a waitress. I don't know that I would do that again; I hated it. But I might, if such a man were to come along." She then watched Preacher for his response.

A few long seconds passed by as Preacher seemed to consider what Bonnie had revealed to him. Then in a soft but firm tone he replied.

"You and Clyde are wanted dead or alive, but mostly dead Bonnie. They say you'll both be shot on sight the first chance the law gets. You're in fairly bad shape already. Your leg needs medical attention. You can't walk very far without someone's help. Do you really believe you can ever 'start fresh' again?"

Bonnie stared at Preacher with disdain. She appeared as if she were about to cry. Then slowly her face became stretched and lifeless. With a cold voice she began to speak begrudgingly, as if the words were struggling to get out.

"Get away from me. Get away from me right now. I don't want to ever speak to you again."

Preacher seemed saddened by this.

"Bonnie, it's the truth. I'm sorry, but it's the truth."

"Did you hear me? I said to get away from me. I don't want to hear anything you have to say." Now her voice became louder. "Get away from me!"

Preacher stood and walked back over to where he sat before just as Henry came around the corner of the house.

Henry looked at Bonnie curiously.

"Give me another cigarette Henry." She said.

He pulled a cigarette from his pack and quickly put it in her outstretched hand.

She instantly lit the cigarette from her previous one with a shaking hand and took a long and desperate drag from it. Then she looked back at Henry as the smoke expelled from her mouth and nostrils.

Henry seemed to wonder if she was all right but neither said anything.

Preacher sat with his legs crossed and laid his coat across his legs.

Soon Clyde came back and sat beside Bonnie. They all sat quietly as the cicadas screeched a constant tune in the trees around them. Henry found some cans of food in the car and they ate from the cans.

As the afternoon turned to evening, Clyde motioned for them to leave and soon the sedan was back on the road.

The sun dropped below the horizon as they pulled into the drive of Henry's father's house. Clyde walked around the car and just as Preacher began to get out he took hold of the door.

"Nope," he said as he lifted a pair of handcuffs. He motioned for Preacher to move to the back seat behind the driver side, and then put one side on Preacher's wrist in the handcuffs and the other handcuff around the window frame of the car.

"I'm getting sick and tired of looking at you." He clicked the handcuffs closed on the door.

Preacher watched in silence as Clyde did this. But as Clyde began to walk away, Preacher replied. "You may not want to look at me anymore Clyde. But it won't change the fact that I'm here."

Clyde glanced back at Preacher but then quickly moved around to help Bonnie.

Henry's father appeared somewhat happy to see his son again. They all laughed about something as they went up the steps to the house.

Henry's father waited until the others were in. He then turned and looked out to where Preacher sat. He expressed concern as he stared in Preacher's direction. Then he turned back to the house and walked inside.

Outside, in the darkness, Preacher listened and stared at the dim light streaming from the windows. Laughter would erupt, and from the sounds and what little could be seen he determined they were playing cards and drinking.

He sat alone quietly. Clyde had done enough in restricting him from any interference. Apparently, he reminded them of things they wished to not think of.

He moved a little to get comfortable. The hours slowly slipped by. He placed his ragged coat behind his head and tried to rest.

Later, more laughter and noises of people walking out of the house aroused Preacher. Clyde and then Bonnie came out the door almost stumbling down the steps. Henry and his father walked out of the door behind them.

"Come on. I want to go for a drive. I'm sick of being in the house." Bonnie sounded about half intoxicated.

"That is a great idea Sugar." Clyde replied, not sounding very sober himself.

They moved toward the car and Preacher sat up. When Clyde reached the car he noticed Preacher and suddenly seemed to lose his humor.

Rather than helping Bonnie in the back he asked her if she would rather sit in the front for a while.

"Yeah, that sounds good. I'm getting tired of riding in the back anyway." After saying this Bonnie crawled into the front seat with Clyde's help.

Henry got into the driver's seat and started the car. Clyde unlocked Preacher and then shut his door, then walked around the back of the car and got in the back seat behind Bonnie and beside Preacher.

He looked over at Preacher with a foreboding in his eyes. Preacher pulled his coat from behind his neck and laid it across his legs.

As the sedan rumbled down the gravel roads Clyde would glance over at Preacher. As he pulled a drag from his cigarette, Clyde's face would light up enough to show an ominous expression. Then Bonnie would laugh about something and Clyde would temporarily turn his attention back to Bonnie.

As the night wore on Preacher pulled his coat up over him and leaned back in the corner between the door and the back seat. He closed his eyes as the others talked and drank.

Cigarette smoke swirled around his nose as all three outlaws smoked one cigarette after the other. He drifted into a light slumber and tried to find solace in the vibration of the car as he also attempted to tune out the loud criminals.

Sometime later, Preacher was aroused from his light sleep by the sudden jolt of the car. As he woke up he realized the vehicle must have hit a bump or pothole in the road.

A strange quiet inside the car indicated the three criminals had finally become exhausted. He laid his head back into the corner and glanced over to Clyde.

Clyde sat leaning in the opposite corner of the car in a similar fashion to Preacher. He stared at Preacher with an evil intent. In his hand he held his pistol pointed at Preacher. The rough road caused the barrel of the pistol to waver slightly, but Clyde sat silent, staunchly aiming it straight at Preacher.

He examined the situation while he lay in the corner. He said nothing but gazed into Clyde's eyes. The young outlaw appeared to be desperate and searching for something unseen.

Preacher knew there was little left to say to Clyde which he'd not already said. He waited and watched.

After what seemed to be many minutes, Clyde began to speak in a low and scornful voice.

"What am I to do about you? I thought if I brought you along, you might help us, but you're no good to me."

Preacher thought a few seconds before replying. Then he spoke in a calm tone.

"It's not my help you want Clyde. You want to manipulate me. You want me to present something false in order to help you justify your actions. Regardless of what you decide to do about me. I won't be beaten down and turned into a living lie."

Clyde now appeared to consider the words before replying, "If you got no use for me, then I got no concern about you."

"There's still time Clyde."

The outlaw seemed puzzled by Preacher's words.

"Time for what?"

"Time to do the right thing," Preacher replied.

This only seemed to anger Clyde even more. He turned slightly to speak to Henry.

"What time is it, Henry?"

Henry acknowledged Clyde's question by a nod. He pulled a cigarette lighter from his jacket pocket and lit it. Then he held it over his watch as he tried to check the time and steer the car. After a few seconds of glancing at his watch Henry answered Clyde.

"It's twelve minutes till midnight."

Clyde looked back at Preacher. He cocked the hammer of the pistol back.

"There's no more time." Clyde pulled the trigger.

The inside of the car lit up as the loud gunshot rang out. The car slid to a halt as Henry slammed on the breaks. Bonnie awoke in a shock and sat up quickly. After realizing they were not being shot at, she instantly became angry.

"Clyde… how many times do I have to tell you to quit that? It makes my leg hurt!"

The back door opened, and Preacher fell limp from the car, rolling into the ditch. The door slammed shut and the car sped away into the darkness.

Dawn broke slowly over the horizon and as the warm sun rose higher into the sky a snake crawled cautiously alongside the road and past the motionless body in the ditch. Cicadas began screeching, individually at first, until slowly a chorus of their strange calls erupted in the trees.

Preacher stirred. Slowly he picked himself up. Sitting in the ditch he looked down and carefully examined himself for damage.

He then examined the ragged coat that he had over him when Clyde pulled the trigger. Lifting it up he identified a bullet entrance on one side and the exit on the other side, indicating a bullet passing through the coat but somehow missing him.

After studying his coat, Preacher moved a little farther from the ditch and closer to the cooler shade of a nearby tree. He sat staring out at the barren road. The cicadas became even louder as the sun crept higher into the sky. Still Preacher sat silently staring at the road.

The sun overhead indicated a time of around 10:00 am and the cicadas now screeched with an unrelenting roar of sound. The road silently mocked Preacher as nothing and no one crossed it all morning.

Then, with a shocking urgency the cicadas fell silent. Nothing could be heard. The slight breeze seemed to have also died.

Preacher gazed around but made no move. The eerie silence held true as seconds ticked by.

Then, he slowly stood up and walked to the side of the dusty road. With the battered coat on his arm he put his hands into his pockets and turned to stare down the rugged gravel lane.

Now the cicadas slowly began to screech again. The breeze once again floated slowly through the air and the leaves in the trees fluttered about in a carefree manner.

After a few moments, the sound of a car could be heard. Then it came into view. Preacher watched as it approached. It swerved a little from one side of the road to the other. He stood fast by the road, not moving.

The automobile passed by him and slowed down. Again, it swerved and after traveling about a quarter mile the car suddenly slid to a stop beside the road.

Preacher turned and began walking toward the vehicle.

The door opened and a large man in a white suit slid halfway out of the car. As Preacher got closer, he watched him with interest.

The man held his chest while leaning over, obviously laboring for breath. He stared at the ground between his feet as he held the place on his chest where his heart would be.

Preacher approached the man and could see he was sweating profusely.

"Are you all right?"

The man turned to Preacher with a taut red face and fear still stretched across it. He then moved his hand inside his suit pocket and pulled out a handkerchief as if to hide the fact he was holding his chest. He wiped his face gingerly with the handkerchief.

"Yeah, I'm fine."

The man stood with some effort. He leaned on the car and tried to pull himself together.

"It's fiercely hot. I just needed to catch my breath."

Preacher studied the man who appeared to be in his late fifties.

"You headed this way?" The man asked this with a feeble point from his hand.

"Yes, I'm headed that way."

"Come on then. There's no need for you to be out here in the heat, all alone like an orphan."

After saying this he chuckled a little and got back into the driver's seat.

Preacher walked around and climbed into the passenger seat across from the man.

As the car began to move down the road Preacher sat watching the man in a concerned manner as he wiped his forehead often with the handkerchief.

Initially he paid little attention to Preacher. Then, as time went by he seemed to feel better. After a while he started to talk.

"This heat reminds me of a week I spent in New Orleans." He looked over at Preacher and smiled, then continued.

"We had a meeting back in, oh 1920 I believe it was. My partner wanted to go to the Red-Light district. He says to me, 'Leonard, we need to go get us a city woman for the night. The wives will never know a thing.'" Then Leonard laughed and looked at Preacher slyly.

"So, we went to the Red Light district and let me tell you, I got hold of a sweet young whore. She said she was twenty-one. But I don't think she could have been over seventeen!" He laughed again.

"She wasn't so sweet when I got done with her though!" He smiled as if reminiscing and then wiped the sweat from his brow as he glanced over at Preacher.

Preacher gave no expression as he simply sat listening to Leonard, who now appeared very excited to speak his mind.

As the car rolled down the dusty roads Leonard became more revealing, and he confessed with zeal many things to Preacher.

"And he hung in that tree for three days before any of them blacks were brave enough to cut him down. I know for sure, because I went by and checked. You see that's what the Klan is there for; to make sure they don't get too high and mighty."

Leonard expressed pride in the dark things he disclosed to Preacher.

As he spoke, Preacher listened intently but gave no sign of approval nor disapproval. This in turn appeared to make Leonard feel at ease because Preacher didn't object to his deeds.

An hour passed by and Leonard had spoken almost without ceasing the entire time.

Then, they suddenly came upon a mass of cars pulled over to the side of the road. People walked toward something ahead and a few were walking away from the mysterious attraction.

Leonard slowed down and pulled over to the side.

"What in H E double L?" He said this with astonishment as people moved by his window.

When a man passed by in the opposite direction as if he had already seen what lay ahead, Leonard asked him. "What's going on up there?"

The man stopped and moved closer to Leonard's window.

"They gunned down Bonnie and Clyde up the road a bit. The law caught 'em in an ambush. A sheriff and some deputies must have plugged 'em a thousand times. There's blood everywhere. It is like a slaughterhouse!"

When the man said this Leonard immediately became excited and a smile erupted across his face.

"You don't say, Bonnie and Clyde? I've got to see this."

The man shook his head a little as if feeling ill. "It's a bloody mess. I ain't ever seen anything like it." He then left in the direction he was going before Leonard stopped him.

Leonard opened the door and got out. He looked over to the passenger seat with an anxious expression.

"Ain't you coming to see?"

Preacher said nothing for a few seconds, and then shook his head with an expression of sadness indicating he didn't intend on going.

"Don't you want to see this?" Leonard asked again with some bewilderment.

"Why would any decent person be eager to see such a thing Leonard?"

The smile faded as Leonard considered this. "Well, this is Bonnie and Clyde though; the outlaws."

Preacher stared at Leonard a few seconds.

"They were still human beings."

Now Leonard's eyes dropped as he seemed to be searching for something else. His face twisted a little as he appeared to see something inside himself that was unattractive.

He looked briefly back to the passenger's seat.

"Well, the truth is, I don't ordinarily like to see this sort of stuff. It's not that I enjoy other people's pain."

Preacher looked him straight into the eyes and the two men remained in this state briefly before Preacher finally spoke.

"Is that the truth, Leonard? Is that the real truth?"

Leonard expressed shame on his face now. He turned away from Preacher and stared at the ground briefly. Yet he gave no answer. He then slowly closed the car door and turned to join the mass of people.

Preacher sat alone, as the multitude moved eagerly to the place of the dead.

The End

We hope you enjoyed Into the Crimson Mist and Twelve Minutes till Midnight. You may also be interested in Ever the Wayward Sky by Oliver Phipps. For your convenience we've added a preview of Ever the Wayward Sky and listed some of his other works here.

EVER THE WAYWARD SKY

Oliver Phipps

Chapter One:

THE WAR IS OVER, BUT THERE'S NO END IN SIGHT

A light haze lay over the North Carolina ground. Sergeant James Taft stepped out of an officer's tent.

"Yes Sir, I will, first thing this afternoon." He replied while moving from the entrance.

As soon as he was completely outside, he became aware of something unusual. The low sound of cheering began to erupt on the far side of the camp. Sergeant Taft turned toward the strange sounds just as his lieutenant stepped out from the tent behind him.

Both men were around the same height and build; five foot ten inches, more or less. However, Sergeant Taft had short dark hair that wasn't curly and unruly as the lieutenants' was. And James also wore a mustache and goatee, which was popular among the Union cavalrymen.

"What's going on, Sergeant?" The lieutenant moved up beside James, and both watched as a spontaneous celebration appeared to be overtaking the entire camp.

"I don't know, Sir. But it seems to be moving this way." As Sergeant Taft said this, soldiers walked at a rapid pace closer to the two men. They yelled and shouted along the way. One man came swiftly toward them, waving his hat and cheering loudly.

"What's going on soldier?" The lieutenant asked when the man came closer.

"Lee surrendered, Sir. He surrendered to General Grant." Then the man jogged away, shouting and jumping as he went.

The lieutenant looked at Sergeant Taft, who looked back at him. They both seemed to be in disbelief. Then, as more and more soldiers came running through the camp shouting, both men began to smile. They turned and shook hands; congratulating each other for surviving.

James Taft had seldom thought or believed the war would end. After more than four years of fighting, he had a difficult time accepting this reality. As the next few weeks went by, however, the twenty-three-year-old sergeant began to accept that he had indeed survived the war.

Eventually, his unit, the 9th Pennsylvania cavalry began to muster out in Kentucky.

"What are you going to do now, Sergeant?" A young private asked James as they left the headquarters building. Sergeant Taft examined his discharge papers. He seemed to be a bit confused and disoriented.

"I'm not sure, private."

"You're not sure? Ain't you going home, sergeant?"

"I suppose I will. What are you going to do?"

The private laughed. "Oh, I got so many things I'm going to do! The first thing is, I'm going to marry my sweetheart, Dolly. Oh, she is a beauty! You got a sweetheart, Sergeant?"

James glanced at the young man.

"No, I don't suppose that I do, Private."

The young man laughed again. "You should get you a sweetheart."

The man stayed with James as they turned in gear and finished other various tasks to complete their discharge. He spoke with almost no restraint. James didn't care though as his mind was absent of anything to talk about.

He felt lost as he said goodbye to his horse. He felt naked as he turned in his revolver and rifle. The saber he'd bought with his money, he gladly packed it with his other meager belongings.

James couldn't seem to break away from the numbness that had taken over him. During his trip home to Pennsylvania, he again became lost in thought. He remembered those he knew that had died in battle. He considered the men he had killed in combat. They wouldn't be going home, ever. They still lay on the battlefield in the cold earth. The war was over. Why couldn't he be glad like so many others? Why did he feel that he shouldn't be leaving the army and yet at the same time, feel that he could not endure any more of the savage brutality he had gone through for four and a half years?

His hometown presented a celebratory atmosphere as James stepped off the train. Banners were hung all around, welcoming the victorious soldier's home.

"James, James Taft! Welcome, home James! My, my, I barely recognized you. You were, what, eighteen when you enlisted? You've grown into quite the man, and hero for that matter."

"Thank you, Mr. Carleton." James shook the man's outstretched hand as a small band struck up the Battle Cry of Freedom. A few of the town women handed out baked items, and one of them poured a cup of black coffee for him.

He looked over the small train station as he sipped the coffee. It hadn't changed much over the years. Yet everything seemed different now.

An elderly lady approached him.

"Your mama is going to be so happy to see you, James! She came down here several times hoping you would arrive with some of the other boys that were coming home. But you've all been coming home a few at a time now after the main group returned."

James smiled at the woman; she had aged considerably in appearance since he last saw her.

"Yes Mrs. Johnson, the cavalry had some extended duties to perform. It took a bit longer for us to muster out."

"Well, no matter. I know she'll be very happy to see you. We're all so proud of you boys."

Mrs. Johnson then took her small handkerchief and put it close to her eye. "It's just a shame we lost so many good young men to that," she acted as if she wanted to say something else, but then continued, "that, terrible war."

James tried to sound compassionate. "Yes Mrs. Johnson, I agree."

"Well James, you tell your mother and the rest of your family hello for me. And we're just so glad to have you back."

Mrs. Johnson then went to speak with another soldier that had also returned on the train.

James moved out of the station and began walking through the Pennsylvania town that he'd grown up in. Memories rushed back to him as he passed buildings and landmarks. Some of the memories brought feelings of his father, who had died when James was only fourteen.

"James? It surely is young James Taft!" An elderly man in an old suit came up quickly to him with an excited expression on his face.

"Hello, Dr. Weston," James said with not nearly as much excitement as he shook the extended doctors' hand.

"James, it is so good to have you back. I'm sorry you didn't get the big parade and all. We had a big to do when our boys from the regiment returned. I wish you could have come home to that."

"It's alright Doc. Mr. Carleton and some of the ladies met us at the station."

"Well, that's good, James. We've tried to have someone at the station as you boys continue to come in."

"I believe we'll be some of the last, Doc," James replied.

The doctor looked down and shook his head a little. "It seems we've lost so many." Then he glanced back up to James. "Do you need a ride out to your place? I can have the horses hooked up to my carriage."

James smiled. "Thank you, Doc, but I would like to walk. I could use a good long stroll."

"Alright James, I understand."

As he moved on out of town and toward his boyhood home, a dark feeling came over him. He gazed over at the "swimming hole" that he and his brother John had swum many times in. Now the laughter he remembered seemed so far away. His heart felt as if it could no longer recover such a joyful time. The death he had seen and dealt with now anchored him to a place neither high nor low. He simply existed.

He continued toward the family home and memories fluttered through his mind. Races with his brother and friends; some of whom now lay buried in the earth of a distant battlefield. Still, James couldn't shake off the darkness to receive the warm thoughts he desired. Maybe, the sight of his home and his mother would stir the embers of joy that he hoped were still in his heart, somewhere.

Slowly the two-story house came into view. As James moved closer, he became frightened. He slowed down and felt a sense of dread. How could a man who had been in more battles than he could recall be terrified of returning home?

James stopped. He stood at a distance from the house. As his heart raced, his mind struggled for an answer. Slowly, the problem began to unravel as he searched his very soul. The questions revealed their ugly presence in his thoughts.

Would they see the terrible things? Would his mother sense the blood and death on him? Would his nephew and niece feel the heat of the hell he had passed through, time and time again? Surely, they would know. He started walking again but felt the weight of these concerns with every step he took. Sweat dripped along the side of his head as these thoughts entrenched themselves into his fears.

With the reluctance, he had felt before racing into a battle, James forced himself to continue moving forward. The aging house came into view as did his niece who was outside. She had grown much since the last time he had seen her. The years had changed her dramatically from the four-year-old girl he remembered. She had her back to him and was kneeled over, picking wildflowers.

James stood outside the small wooden fence that was in obvious need of repairs. He watched his niece in silence as she hummed and picked the flowers one by one. He felt himself trembling in anticipation of her noticing him. Would she scream in fear? Would she see the things he had been through and cry from sadness?

He wanted to do something to let her know that he was behind her, but he felt too frightened to do anything. Then, as she turned, she noticed him standing outside the fence. She stared at him for several seconds with a slightly startled expression. James smiled a little smile at her.

"Uncle James?" She took several small steps toward him as she asked this.

"Hello, Grace." He said to her, relieved that she couldn't see the wariness inside him.

Grace cautiously walked over to the fence. She then extended her handful of flowers to him. James took the flowers and softly said. "Thank you."

"We've been waiting for you Uncle James." As she said this, James' mother stepped out to the front porch and immediately put her hand to her mouth and began to weep.

"James...!" She moved quickly down the porch toward him. His brother now came out and then his wife, with their son behind her. All of them began to say his name and rush to hug him.

Later, he sat in the main room. Everyone sat around him as if he was about to tell a grand tale. His sister-in-law brought him a drink.

"We've been hoping you would show up any day now James." His brother John said and then continued.

"Ma waited at the train station again and again when the regiment began to arrive, but no one could tell us anything about the 9th. We finally stopped going to the station. No one seemed to know anything about the cavalry."

James took a drink and sat the glass on a table beside him.

"Well, we had some extra duties to take care of. We watched over some of the larger reb units as they surrendered. I didn't know how long it would be or I would have written and let everyone know."

His mother appeared to glow from joy.

"No matter, James. We're just so happy to have you back, son."

"Yeah, James, we'll get this place back into shape in no time with you back!" His brother John added.

James smiled a little. He felt strangely out of place sitting peacefully with his family.

"Yeah, we'll do that John." He picked up his drink, more from being nervous than needing it.

As he took a sip, his mind searched for the reason he felt so uncomfortable. He didn't want to talk about farming. He didn't want to think about getting the place back into shape. He felt depressed even considering these things.

Then, with no warning, his nephew Johnny unexpectedly asked a question.

"Did you kill a bunch of Reb's Uncle James?"

John immediately reprimanded his son as everyone looked around in shock.

"Johnny, don't ask such a thing!"

"Why Pa, I want to know?"

A strange sensation swept over James, and he had to get up. He then replied with obvious discomfort, "That's alright, John... I think I'll get some air for a few minutes."

He left the room as the others tried to explain to young Johnny why he shouldn't ask such questions. James stepped out onto the porch and sat down on the steps, in the dark.

His heart beat rapidly. He realized something terrible now. Only when Johnny asked him that question did he feel alive again. What was wrong with him? He ran his fingers through his hair.

John stepped out on the porch behind him. He sat down beside his younger brother.

"I'm sorry James. He's just... so young."

"No, it's alright. I just needed some air. I'm not used to being inside. We slept under the stars as much as we did anywhere else."

John glanced over at his brother. He took a deep breath of the moist night air.

"I wanted to join up, but with Pa gone and two young children."

"No... John. You did the right thing. You're the real soldier for taking care of Ma and this place. I'm sorry that I ran off and left you like I did. I had visions of being some hero, I suppose."

The two men sat quietly for a few minutes and stared out over the dark fields in front of them. Then John said with a softened voice.

"Sounds like your unit had it pretty rough. Up against Forrest and Morgan, seems the 9th took on some of the toughest."

"Yeah, I guess we got our share of it," James replied.

"Well, at least you didn't leave anything out there on the battlefield." John then slapped James on the leg. He stood up and walked back into the house. James then said in a small voice, to himself.

"I'm not so sure of that."

As the days passed, James felt himself sinking further into depression. He tried to work on the family farm but couldn't focus on the tasks. Darkness slowly began to swallow him from the inside out.

"Well, we finally pulled that old stump out of the South field." John attempted to sound encouraging at the dinner table.

"That's wonderful. That old tree always irritated your Pa. I'm glad we took care of it, and it's gone for good." His mother glanced over at James after saying this.

Her son sat staring blankly at his plate of food. He heard nothing they had said.

His mother turned and looked across the table at John, who then glanced over at his wife, Velma. All three now watched James as he held his fork over his food and appeared to be far away.

The two children took notice of what was occurring and began watching their Uncle also.

Realizing the children were watching, Velma stood up and took a pitcher of water over to James.

"Would you like some more water, James?"

He almost shook as he came out of the apparent trance.

"Oh, no Velma, thank you."

Johnny laughed a little, and this caused Grace to giggle as well.

"You children eat now. No playing."

"Yes, Grandma." Both children replied, almost in unison.

James looked around the table with a lost expression on his face.

"I think it'll rain tonight," John said to bring supper back on track. "What do you think James?"

"Yes, it might."

He knew something wasn't right. He realized now that he'd been somewhere else. He didn't know what to do about it, though. He glanced around at his family. He loved them dearly, but he didn't belong here. He wasn't sure where he belonged, but he knew now that it wasn't here.

Later, as James lay down to sleep, the rain began. The soft pattering of raindrops outside his window caused a soothing effect, and he drifted into sleep. Then the thunder came, and as James slipped farther into slumber, he found himself on a faraway battlefield again. As the sounds of the storm erupted outside, the cannons roared on the battlefield of James' dream.

"I heard them was Morgan's boys over there, Sergeant."

A young private nervously spoke to Sergeant Taft, who was riding back and forth in front of the men. James reined his horse in to answer the young cavalryman.

"Don't matter who they are, private! That cavalry unit is protecting the Reb's flank, and we'll run them off the battlefield, or die trying!"

When James said this, the private appeared to calm down. But he was still obviously frightened. All the soldiers appeared concerned. The horses moved underneath them nervously; sensing death to be close at hand. Smoke from the guns drifted through the unit's ranks as James scanned the faces of his men.

He then moved closer to the young private. James thought he might be able to say something to calm the young man, but as he came near, the soldier began to speak.

"I sure got the feeling that I'm going to be one of those that die trying, Sergeant. You ever get that feeling?"

James reined in his mount again, trying to calm it. The horse quivered under him in an apprehensive excitement for the battle at hand. Then, James lied to the young private. He always lied in these situations.

"Almost every day, private." After James had said this, the man calmed some more. He smiled a little. James smiled slightly as well, and then he thought of several other men that had told him the same sort of thing over the years. They all died on the battlefield after telling him this. The cracking of rifle and cannon fire became intense. He positioned his horse to the front of the unit, ready for battle.

Their lieutenant rode swiftly up from the back of the unit.

"Alright boys, it's time, let's give'em hell."

The lieutenant then pulled his saber out and nodded to their bugler, who immediately sounded the charge. Sergeant Taft spurred his horse just as the lieutenant charged forward.

"Let's go 9th," James yelled out, and his heart began to pound inside his chest.

The ground began to tremble as the horses burst into a gallop.

James looked across the field at the enemy just as bullets began to sing around him.

He became hot as the blood rushed to his head. Then, as always, he slowly became numb as the specter of death approached.

He put the reins in his mouth and lowered his head as if facing a fierce wind. He could now see the enemy's faces clearly.

As the gap closed, he pulled his saber out with his left hand and his revolver out with his right.

The famed "Rebel yell" could be heard from the opposing forces, sending chills down his back.

Now everything began to happen at lightning speed. The two cavalry units collided with the ferocity of a train wreck. As he moved into the Confederates' ranks, he swung his razor-sharp saber and took a Rebels' head almost entirely off from the shoulders. He then turned to his left and fired his pistol into the chest of another, removing the man from his horse in the process.

The sound of bullets flying by him mixed with bodies being struck and cries of pain, all mingled with anger, leather, and metal striking metal.

Another rebel rode up to his right. He was young, and James could see the fear in his eyes. He fired his pistol, but James anticipated it just in time to move. The bullet whizzed by so close that he felt the heat. He maneuvered his saber as the young soldier attempted to cock his pistol again. He lunged the blade forward and felt the steel sink into the man's body. He watched briefly as the soldier realized James had just ended his life.

He pulled the blade from the man and turned to his left as another soldier was about to fire his rifle at him. James quickly aimed and instinctively fired his cocked pistol. The soldier leaned back as the bullet hit him, firing the gun into the air before falling from his horse.

The enemy was all around him now. He shot another Rebel from his horse. Another one rode toward him as if to avenge his comrade. James shot him also as he tried to swing his saber.

He wanted to get out of the enclosed fighting. He maneuvered his mount to the right, then ran another rebel through the back with his saber. He struggled to pull the blade free as the soldier fell backward onto it.

A bullet cut through the side of his coat contacting his flesh. He remained on top of his horse. He spotted the enemy that fired the shot. He aimed his revolver and shot as the soldier tried to shoot again. James' shot almost removed the soldier's head.

He pressed his right arm against the wounded side as the pain came. Angered, he spurred his horse forward. He swung his blade and the contact nearly took a passing rebel's arm off.

Another rebel rode toward him at a furious pace, seeming ready to take James down with his saber. James lifted his pistol and shot him from his horse. Then he immediately ran his blade into the side of another rebel that had moved close to him.

James sensed another enemy soldier taking aim; the shot intended for the young private he had spoken with before the start of the battle. James lifted his pistol and pulled the trigger. The clicking of an empty revolver was all he heard. As the young private turned, he would see the bullet from the enemy that would kill him. James yelled out.

"Noooo...!!"

He cocked the pistol again as the rebel fired. The young private jerked back as the bullet slammed into his chest. James again pulled the trigger; again, and again, the clicking of an empty pistol.

"James?"

The Rebel then turned toward him, and everything slowed down. James raised his saber as the hot blood flowed to his head and caused a flash of anger inside him.

"James, are you alright?"

The battlefield began to fade. James slowly saw his room by the light of a lamp that his mother held. He found himself sitting on the edge of his bed. His left arm raised as if he were holding a saber, while his right arm was elevated halfway and pointed from his body in a manner suggesting a pistol ready to be used.

He blinked several times and looked to his mother, who stood in the doorway with a lamp. She appeared very concerned. Then, John stepped up behind her. As James lowered his arms, Grace and Johnny stepped to the door to see what the commotion was. At last, Velma stepped to the door behind John.

"I guess I was dreaming. I'm sorry if I disturbed anyone."

"Come on children; Uncle James just had a dream." His mother attempted to usher the children away from the doorway. John seemed to want to say something but couldn't find the words. Velma turned and went back toward their bedroom. Finally, John spoke in a nervous tone.

"Well, good night James. I'll uh... I'll see you at breakfast." he then waved slightly and left for his bedroom.

James sat in silence on the edge of the bed. His heart continued to race long after everyone had settled back into their beds. He told himself that he hated the battlefield. The smell of smoke and blood still permeated his nostrils, even though it was only a dream. And yet here he sat, on the edge of the bed, in darkness and silence, reliving the vivid dream over and over in his mind. He wanted to be there again, and this frightened him more than any battle ever did.

As the morning light slowly peeked over the horizon, James' mother stepped out onto the porch where her son sat in a weathered chair. He gazed out to the horizon and only glanced away as his mother sat down across from him.

Several minutes had passed before either spoke. His mother began, softly, but seeming to struggle for her words.

"I wish... well, I just wish your father were here, James. He would be so much better with something like this."

James glanced at her and smiled a little. He then turned back to watch the morning sun creeping up. After a few seconds, he spoke with a slow but resolved tone.

"I never really thought about what I would do after the war, Ma. Because I never believed, I would live through it." He paused and his mother looked down a little as if his words pained her some. He then continued with the same tone.

"I can't stay here. This... staying in one place, it's doing something to me. I'm not for certain what, but it's not good, I know that."

His mother continued to gaze down at the porch, appearing to almost cry. After several seconds, she straightened and again spoke softly.

"You shouldn't run from your problems, Son."

He turned to his mother and examined her face. He loved her so much and wanted to make her understand that he had no desire to leave. He tried desperately to find the words. She looked back to her son with a hope that he might be able to stay. But as she gazed into his eyes, James realized what he needed to say.

"I'm not running from them, Ma. I've got to charge them, at full gallop. It's the only thing I know how to do now. I've got to meet them out there... somewhere, and overcome them, or die trying. I don't know what the outcome will be, but I know now what happens if I stay here."

A tear ran down his mother's face as she realized his words were true, and she would once again be losing her son. She put her head down and wiped the tear away. She nodded a little as another tear dropped to her lap.

Later that morning, John approached his brother, who had walked to the creek. James sat on a large rock, the same one the two had used as young boys to jump into the water.

"It's been a long time since you and I went swimming here." John then sat down beside his brother.

James turned and glanced at him. He then looked back to the creek and tossed a small stone in, as if he'd been waiting for a reason to throw it into the water.

"Yeah, feels like a different lifetime. I've been thinking about those days; before..." James acted reluctant to even say the word.

"Before the war..." John said, with the tone of a big brother. He obviously wanted to confront the problem and resolve it.

James sensed this, but knew the problem was not as simple as removing a tree stump.

"Yeah, before the war," he replied without looking up.

Again, the silence prevailed and the soft flowing creek, along with a few birds was the only sounds heard. Finally, John felt the need to say something.

"Ma says you're going to leave?"

James reached down and picked up another small stone, then replied.

"I can't stay here any longer, John. The war did something to me. I don't know what, exactly, but I know I've got to move. If I don't, I'll get sick."

John looked over at his brother and tried to find an answer. He could think of nothing to change his brother's mind. With no solution in sight, he decided to do what he could to be a friend.

"Where are you planning on going to?"

James glanced at John and felt glad his brother was trying to understand. He tossed the small stone into the creek.

"West, there's a lot of room to move around, out that way. I saved most of my pay from the Army, so I should have enough to get me by for a while. I'll give Ma some money before I leave. I know it won't be the same as having an extra hand around, but maybe it'll help some."

John could only nod in agreement. He knew his brother would stay if he were able to. He patted James' leg and stood up.

"Will you be coming to dinner?"

"Yeah, I'll be back later, before dinner."

John nodded and began walking back toward the house. James again stared at the creek, as if it might answer some of the questions in his mind.

As the sun crept up toward noon, James left the small waterway and went back to the house. He decided he would leave as soon as he could get a good horse and the proper equipment together for an extended trip out West.

Over the next several days he purchased a good mount and all the necessary gear, including two brand new Colt Army revolvers and a Henry rifle.

The departure day came, and he said his good-byes, then moved down the road, away from the house where he had grown to be a young man.

Upon reaching the creek, he turned the horse around and looked back at his home in the distance. He didn't want to leave it. But in his heart, James knew he had to. Something inside him would not rest. The battle within had to run its course, somewhere and somehow. Staying here would only worsen the situation and disrupt the family he loved. With this thought in mind, he turned his horse and moved down the road, toward the struggle he knew he must face. Out there, in the West, somewhere, an unseen enemy awaited him.

*

Thank you for reading the preview of Ever the Wayward Sky. Here are some other books by Oliver Phipps that you may be interested in.

Sane Grace

In the year 2054, earth has become an inter-galactic outpost for trade among friendly planets.

The potential rewards in this new era are great, but so are the risks. An alien drug called Fellirex has recently saturated the black market. It's cheap and highly addictive, and in few weeks, half the world's population could become addicts.

From across the globe, the world's finest are gathered to end the smuggling of this drug. Lieutenant Wolfe, a young and attractive special operations officer, seems completely out of place among the heroes and decorated veterans.

Much to the frustration of her commanding officer, she is given an assignment, and her teammate is almost immediately, critically wounded. A detective takes a chance and volunteers to team up with the seemly erratic young woman. However, it is not long before he questions that decision.

Trapped on a wild and hazardous journey across the globe and into space itself, the detective realizes Grace may not be who he thought she was. In fact, Grace herself appears to question her true intentions and motives.

A Tempest Soul

Seventeen-year-old Gina Falcone has been alone for most of her life. Her father passed away while she was young, and her un-affectionate mother eventually leaves her to care for herself when she was only thirteen.

Though her epic journey begins by an almost deadly mistake, Gina will find many of her heart's desires in the most unlikely of places. The loss of everything is the catalyst that brings her to an unimagined level of accomplishment in her life.

However, Gina, soon realizes it is the same events that brought her success that may also bring everything crashing down around her. The new life she has built soon beckons for something she left behind. Now, the new woman must find a way to dance through a life she could have never dreamt of.

Where the Strangers Live

When a passenger plane disappeared over the Indian Ocean in autumn 2013, a massive search gets underway.

A deep trolling, unmanned pod picks up faint readings, and soon the deep-sea submersible Oceana and her three crew members are four miles below the ocean surface in search of the black box from flight N340.

Nothing could have prepared the submersible crew for what they discover and what happens afterward. Ancient evils and other world creatures challenge the survival of the Oceana's crew. Mysteries of the past are revealed, and death hangs in the balance for Sophie, Troy and Eliot in this deep-sea Science Fiction thriller.

Twelve Minutes till Midnight

A man catches a ride on a dusty Louisiana road, only to find out he's traveling with notorious outlaws Bonnie and Clyde.

The suspense is nonstop as confrontation settles in, between a man determined to stand on truth, and an outlaw determined to dislocate him from it.

"Twelve Minutes till Midnight will take you on an unforgettable ride."

Diver Creed Station

Wars, diseases, and a massive collapse of civilization have ravaged the human-race of a hundred years in the future. Finally, in the late twenty-second century, mankind slowly begins to struggle back from the edge of extinction.

When a huge "virtual life" facility is restored from a hibernation type of storage and slowly brought back online, a new hope materializes.

Fragments of humanity begin to move into the remnants of Denver and the Virtua-Gauge facilities, which offer seven days of virtual leisure for seven days work in this new and growing social structure.

Most inhabitants of this new lifestyle begin to hate the real world, and work for the seven-day period inside the virtual pods. It's the variety of luxury role play inside the virtual zone that supply's the incentive needed to work hard for seven days in the real world.

In this new social structure, a man can work for seven days in a food dispersal unit and earn seven days as a twenty-first century software billionaire in the virtual zone. As time goes by, and more of the virtual pods are brought back online life appears to be getting better.

Rizette and her husband Oray are young technicians that settle into their still-new marriage as the virtual facilities expand and thrive.

Oray has recently attained the level of a Class A Diver and enjoys his job. The Divers are skilled technicians that perform critical repairs to the complex system, from inside the virtual zone.

His occupation as a Diver demands constant work in the secure "lower levels" of the system. These highly secure areas are the dividing space between the real world and the world of the virtual zone. When the facility was built, the original designers intentionally placed this buffer zone in the programming to avoid threats from non-living virtual personnel.

As Oray becomes more experienced in his elite technical position as a Diver, he is approached by his virtual assistant and forced to make a difficult decision. Oray's decision triggers events that soon pull him and his wife Rizette into a deadly quest for survival.

The stage becomes a massive and complex maze of virtual world sequences, as escape or entrapment hang on precious threads of information.

System ghosts from the distant past, intermingle with mysterious factions that have thrown Oray and Rizette into a cyberspace trap with little hope for survival.

Ghosts of Company K: Based on a True Story

Tag along with young Bud Fisher during his daily adventures in this ghostly tale based on actual events. It's 1971 and Bud and his family move into an old house in Northern Arkansas. Bud soon discovers they live not far from a very interesting cave and a historic Civil War battle site. As odd things start to happen, Bud tries to solve the mysteries, but soon the entire family experiences a haunting situation.

If you enjoy ghost tales based on true events, then you'll enjoy Ghosts of Company K. This heartwarming story brings the reader into the life and experiences of a young boy growing up in the early 1970s. Seen through innocent and unsuspecting eyes, Ghosts of Company K reveals a haunting tale from the often-unseen perspective of a young boy.

Bane of the Innocent

"There's no reason for them to shoot us; we ain't anyone" - Sammy, Bane of the Innocent.

Two young boys become unlikely companions during the fall of Atlanta. Sammy and Ben somehow find themselves, and each other, in the rapidly changing and chaotic environment of the war-torn Georgia City.

As the siege ends and the fall begins in late August and early September of 1864, the Confederate troops begin to move out, and Union forces cautiously move into the city. Ben and Sammy simply struggle to survive, but in the process, they develop a friendship that will prove more important than either could imagine.

A Life Naïve

Life for twenty-seven-year-old Hershel Lawson has been relatively uneventful, and that's the way he likes it. When his grandmother passes away, leaving him her car and a last wish of him taking her ashes to L.A., his life takes a turn and it will never be the same again.

With his new task and grandmother's ashes, Hershel sets out from St. Louis Missouri in the spring of 1962. He travels unimpeded along scenic Route 66 for two days, but is suddenly and unexpectedly relieved of two important things, his car and wallet.

Sally is a sassy and street-smart young woman on her way to Hollywood. She's determined to prove everyone wrong in the "one horse town" she left and be successful as an actress in California. Through mishaps of her own, Sally comes across Hershel. Though neither one realizes it, the real journey is about to begin.

Take a seat and journey with Hershel and Sally along historic Route 66 during its heyday. Laugh and maybe shed a tear or two as they struggle against the odds, and often each other, to make it a few more miles down the highway.

The Bitter Harvest

It's 1825, and a small Native American village has lost many of its people and bravest warriors to a pack of Lofa; huge beasts' humanoid in shape and covered with coarse hair. The creatures are taller than any normal man, and fiercer than even the wildest animal.

Rather than leave the land of their ancestors, the tribe chooses to stay and fight the beasts. But they're losing the war, and perhaps more critically, they're almost without hope.

The small community grasps for anything to help them survive. There is a warrior on the frontier known as Orenda. He's already legendary across the west for his bravery and honor.

Onsi, a young villager, sets out on a journey to find the warrior.

Orenda will be forced to choose between almost certain death, not just for himself, but also his warrior wife Nazshoni and her brother Kanuna, or a dishonorable refusal that would mean annihilation for the entire village.

The crucial decision is only the beginning, and Orenda will soon face the greatest test of his life; the challenge that could turn out to be too much even for a legendary warrior.

Into the Crimson Mist

From the tales of Orenda, book two. This is the sequel to The Bitter Harvest.

After a long winter encampment, Orenda, Nazshoni, Kanuna and Onsi cross the Mississippi river and venture west. Their destination is far and Orenda intends to move the small group of warriors with haste in the hope of reaching an embattled tribe far to the west of the great river.

The plan begins to unravel when they come across a ghost village and then dire forebodings from an old Shaman. There is a shapeshifter in the area, and she has been causing much destruction and despair. Orenda attempts to go around the troubled area as he feels tomahawks and arrows are no match against magic. But the Deer Woman is already aware of the warrior's presence in her territory.

If you enjoyed The Bitter Harvest, you'll not want to miss the continuing adventures of Orenda and his small group of heroes.

Spyder Bones

We've heard the tales. The eternal struggle between good and evil. Many religions are based on the concepts. God, Satan, angels and demons; ideals interwoven into our very existence.

Most people have chosen a side, whether they admit it to themselves or not. Many have at least a basic understanding of what is happening. Some have even discovered secrets beyond the veil of what we see. However, there are a few, who not only understand the war, but are in the very thick of it.

This is the story of Spyder Bones, a mystic warrior.

It's the summer of 1969 and Aaron Prescott is a seasoned soldier. After serving one tour of duty in Vietnam as a cavalryman, Aaron returns for a second tour as a combat medic.

Aaron's life revolves around the love of his Vietnamese girlfriend, the danger of combat, and his passion for music. It's not an overly complicated existence, but that's about to change.

Aaron, or Spyder as he is known to his friends, suffers a near death experience during combat. He is subsequently trapped in a comatose state for months. During this time, he is exposed to an unseen war. A spiritual struggle that most people only have a vague awareness of.

Aaron must make some difficult decisions, but, regardless of anything else, he knows his life will never be the same.

Tears of Abandon

Several college friends start planning a two-week kayak trip down an Alaskan river during late summer 1992. Soon there are five young people headed to Alaska for a river expedition.

As the trip unfolds, and the group gets farther into the wilderness a strange whispering sound attracts their attention. The wonderful vacation begins to take a turn for the worse when they follow the sounds and find something long lost and quite unexpected.

www.ingramcontent.com/pod-product-compliance
Lightning Source LLC
Chambersburg PA
CBHW060625130626
46555CB00002B/662

* 9 7 8 1 9 4 5 5 3 0 9 4 4 *